Christmas Present

Seasonal ghost stories

Pete Hartley

Text copyright © Pete Hartley 2024

All rights reserved.

This is a work of fiction. Names, characters, places, incidents and dialogues are products of the author's imagination or are used fictitiously.

Any resemblance to actual people, living or dead is entirely coincidental.

an **uneasybook**

ISBN: 9798338943625

Christmas Present

Seasonal ghost stories

THIRD EDITION 2024
The proceeds from the sale of this book will be donated to registered charities.

CONTENTS

To Whom It May Concern	1
The Keep	5
Pillion	12
Waiting at the Dray-Horse Inn	17
Home for Christmas	24
The Companion	32
The House	39
The Grammar School	47
Gothic Revival	97
Notes on the Content	104
Also available	106

With thanks to
all those who first saw fit
to commit these tales to print
or to the airwaves;
and to the unseen
who kindly conducted
secret scrutiny
upon them.

PH

Winter 2024

Damp with sweat, mouth is dry
Twisted branches catch the eye
Beside your bed the angel stands
You cannot touch his withered hands.

David Cousins

'Ghosts'

Pete Hartley

TO WHOM IT MAY CONCERN

December 2011

I am well aware of the dangers of walking alone late at night. I do so by choice, frequently, most nights. This is because I cannot sleep; and I'm looking for someone.

If you are tempted to walk home after the bars close my advice is always call a cab, but avoid the horse-drawn Hackney that can sometimes be seen beneath the bridge in Glovers Court at thirteen minutes past three in the morning. I've seen it several times.

I usually start in Church Street. Some of its congregation hold the Minster in their everlasting affections long after their service is over. You may observe them if the moon is three-quarters and the clock is striking too slowly, as it occasionally does in the depth of night.

One such loiterer is the man murdered in St. John's Place, a street that bounds the graveyard of the Minster. James Fell is harmless enough, but we must keep an eye out for his killer. Buck Beardsworth is a much more unsavoury character. He roams widely. Wherever you are now as you read this, he may be standing behind you.

There's a rumour that Buck lies in wait inside the Hackney cab in Glovers Court. He wasn't in there when I rode in it.

There it was. Its lacquered coachwork scuffed by careless customers, its wheels chamfered by cobbles and kerbs, its leather polished by countless coats, its door handle warmed by ever-cold hands. I twisted that handle and climbed inside.

The horseman's whip instantly snapped at the fog, his reins slapped the horses' hide and the brace of steeds kicked away stationary inertia and thrashed out the moving kind. From that instant I saw only Victorian views, as we bounced and jolted over stone sets and ill-repaired roads. I hammered on the underside of the roof and shouted profanities at the coachman, but he ignored me and cursed the geldings towards a gallop.

His cab always comes back without a fare.

The horses raced at breakneck speed but,

despite their supernatural strength, they had to slow as they scaled the incline to Gallows Hill where the English Martyrs church was being built. I took my chance and leaped from the moving cab, and fell to earth without pain or injury. I dusted myself off and stood, and by the time I had done so, the church was finished and the traffic lights had returned to red.

If you ever walk home that way watch out for cars and hope that there are some to keep you company, because if there's none in sight a particular tram may turn up. You can smell the spark from the overhead cable. Don't be tempted to take a north-bound ride. It only goes to the terminus.

I walked towards Fulwood, where she used to live. She is sporadically seen on Plum Pudding Hill I am informed, especially at this time of year, sporting a coat of holly green, with white gloves and a pheasant feather in her hat. I didn't see her that night. I haven't seen her in a long time.

I have it on good authority that she visits the Harris Museum, and I can understand why. It contains the names of some of those that she will have known. I've watched for her there many nights. Some say she even comes by day and they have heard the echo of her cough as she struggles to sustain correct composure. They claim to have felt the draught from her passing as she circles the central void. I think it is more likely that she stands upon the stairs.

I yearn for her. She's looking for me too. I know she is. When she goes into the Harris Museum, she will read my name. It's carved in the wall.

I've told you this in case you should catch sight of her. If you see her, tell her I asked after her. You don't need to say who sent the message. She'll know. It couldn't be anyone else. I hope.

Tell her: the twenty-eighth of December at the Parish Church. This time I'll be there. Meanwhile I'll wassail with my fellow members of the unforgotten guild. Each of us has been untimely robbed. We're sorry if our presence causes you distress. We want you to be happy. That's why we went.

Enjoy yourself, and be generous while you can. There's no time like the present, and vice versa.

THE KEEP

Advent 2011

No one else seemed to notice him but she could see him very clearly. She saw him reflected in the jeweller's window. He was standing behind her and looking over her shoulder at the array of rings, necklaces, bracelets and once-promised but never delivered gifts. She drew a sharp breath and turned to face him.

She focused on the speckles of moisture in the fabric of his frock coat and top hat and then looked deep into the matt glaze of his eyes. He refused to see her. After a chapter of time, he

gave a shallow sigh, turned away and walked off along Fishergate.
She followed.
Why shouldn't she follow him? She was leaving anyway. She had her belongings with her in a single suitcase and he was going in the right direction. Things had gone from bad to beyond worse and she simply couldn't face the festive season. Mother verses daughter. She was going to let mother win. That would beat her.

Her quarry strode ahead with purpose. Pedestrians parted to let him through even though they did not know that he was there. Somehow, they perceived his presence without realising that they did so, and hence a passage opened up for him through the thicket of late-night shoppers. Her senses, on the other hand, were strangely heightened and so she trod a trail of two cities: the globally branded concrete, glass and steel of today, and the cobble, brick and sooty air of a town long gone. She heard the slamming of steam-driven steel and scented a smoky perfume with a distinctly watery high note.

She trailed him to the railway station where he stood on platform two like a monument to himself. He was not quite stationary for his gloved hands toyed with the polished handle of his lacquered walking cane, which he bore in true Victorian fashion, for effect rather than assistance.

They waited in unison. She faced the cold reality. There was no turning back. Was there? She didn't know where she was going, but go she would. Wouldn't she? She'd heard all the warnings when at school not that long ago, but long enough to mean that because she knew the dangers, the dangers wouldn't know her. She hoped.

She felt unhappy about her suitcase. It was imperfectly packed. She felt she was taking too much of her past with her and she wished that instead she could carry enough courage to make a complete break. She'd moved what money she had into a new account and had planned to walk out leaving all but the clothes she needed for the journey but she hadn't been able to summon sufficient strength of spirit. She wanted to rewrite her life from a blank page and felt that the contents of her case belonged to a previous time. It was half-empty but twice as heavy. She felt that she wanted to unburden herself and become a free spirit.

There was no announcement as the thoroughly modern multiple unit slid almost silently into view. Then brakes scuffed, squealed, and gripped and the train stopped with one set of doors exactly opposite the mirrored toe-caps of his shoes.

The carriages were empty and no commuter acknowledged its presence, no anxious traveller inquired as to its destination, no railway worker gave it a glance. The doors opened. The Victorian got on. The train trembled. The doors remained open.

She followed.

She took a seat three behind him. The doors closed, the brakes exhaled, the engine beneath the floor hammered, they drifted forwards, and she left the familiar sodium glow of her home town and slipped into the Bible-hue of the December night.

Ten minutes later the train stopped. The engine purred. The Victorian left his seat and stood in readiness by the door until the button illuminated. He pressed the button and the door opened. She tasted the crystalline draught from the frosted cutting as the man slipped his cane under his arm and climbed down from the carriage.

She followed.

There was no signal at danger. There was nothing on the track. She caught a glimpse of the driver. He looked only at the rails of his route but waited politely, as if inviting her to change her mind but she tightened her grip on her suitcase and stood her ground, and eventually the doors closed and the exhaust pipe unfurled a flag of oily fumes to veil a segment of the heavens as the train found forward momentum and eased away. Soon it was silent, and soon after that it was gone from sight. They were standing on a footpath crossing between two sprung gates. The Victorian traversed the track and passed through the far gate, and she followed after him.

Their path took them immediately into woods laced with the smell of smoke. Cottages, flicker lit by thrifty candles and modestly banked open fires, came into view as dogs growled and shouted and strained at chains secured to eyelets set into the walls. Sallow faces pressed at thick panes as first he, and then she, strode past.

They broke from the wood and followed the line of a crenelated wall until the rising half-moon showed them a door marked 'private'. The

Dickensian pushed at it with splayed gloves until it gave sufficient space for them to pass through.

Inside the enclosure there was less light and more undergrowth and their feet broke stems brittle with ingrained frost and sprung upon paths overgrown due to under-use. They came eventually to a ruined and dilapidated place. Once the guest-house of a king, it was now a farmhouse for an absentee tenant.

"It's worse than I recall," he said. His pronunciation was practised.

"I've never been here before," she said.

"Me neither," he said.

She fixed him with a quizzical stare.

"I don't understand," she said to him. For the first time she felt impelled to touch him, but he was on the move and within a moment they were inside the quadrangle near the more solid ghost of the statue on its plinth. The spectral echo of her breath was rebounded back by the walls. She felt the downdraught of wing beats but saw and heard none. Someone moved across the courtyard behind her and the flagstones spoke of shod hooves. She whipped her head round and a single strand of hair slipped between her lips. She drew it free and found it to be three times the length of hers. No sign of horse or human.

"Over here," said the Victorian from the corner of the courtyard. Strange moans filled the sky and flashes of heat made uncomfortable silhouettes of the walls. She heard drums, dull thuds of air and the shouts of desperate men. A new draught brought the stench of spent gunpowder. "This way," he said, and he hurried away across the courtyard and around to the northern side of the site. She rushed to be near him but stopped dead as a massive structure outperformed all digital animation and built itself before her. It was a defensive tower, robust and proud.

"The Great Keep," he said.

"The what?"

"The Great Keep."

"This?"

"When I wasn't here last, neither was this," he said.

"Sorry?"

He showed her his undertaker's face, half frown half smile, then lifted his gaze in admiration of the fortified edifice new-born and centuries old. After that he tipped his hat, gripped his cane and prepared to leave.

"Wait!" she implored and her suitcase slammed against flagstones heavy with the heritage they endured. She raced to block the path of the Dickensian enigma. "You've brought me here . . ." she said, but he cocked his head askance to interrupt her.

"Have I?"

"Haven't you?"

Voices argued in her head or outside of it, or perhaps nowhere at all.

"We shared a train," he said. "Same tracks, different journey."

"What did you mean when you said you weren't here last time you came?"

He pursed his lips as if picking the pocket of her thoughts. "You can never go back to the same place," he said, "because whenever you return you are always a changed character."

He touched the brim of his top hat again and stepped to one side in a wisp of a waltz. He indicated the keep and looked upon it with a mixture of melancholy and admiration. "Hard times," he said and during the silence that followed she could not tell whether he saw history or memory. Then he gave a snippet of a smile as he formulated his farewell phrase. "We must make the final imprint of the past the first draft of the future." Then he was an olive twist of smoke, and then not even that.

To her left the small door leading into the keep opened. She heard familiar phrases in a half-familiar double-thick accent. She ventured closer, caught the incense of well-cooked stew and heard sentiments she knew. This was a domestic row with public overtones. She understood the sense, for she'd done the Civil War for homework. She was the expert; she knew the arguments and she'd seen the consequences. The tower in front of her was a present from her past. Its permanence was ephemeral. It was a bleak house of great expectation.

She edged her way back to the courtyard. Staring through the entrance arch she could see the twenty-first century. The gates were open, she could walk free and find her way home, or she could answer the call from within.

On the eve of Christmas Eve, they found her suitcase.

PILLION

Winter 1988

The bike growled as if in warning as he released his grip on the throttle. He braked gently expecting ice on the high moorland road. Freezing fog that night, the weatherman had said, and fog there was. Mike was too wise to doubt the other part of the prophesy.

He was sure now that the figure was female. Long hair was common among both sexes of biker, and full leathers could fool, but her stance was undoubtedly feminine. It must have been clear to her that he was slowing but she still held her thumb cocked in arrogant request. He glanced down the length of stone wall at either side of the road, searching in vain for the transport that accompanied the helmet she held in her other hand.

He prepared himself for trickery: an accomplice over the wall. He'd heard of bike thefts like that. When he stopped he put only his right foot down, so that the left was poised to kick the machine into gear. He kept the clutch lever squeezed back and raised his visor with his right hand, but by then the frame had settled as she sat behind him.

Mike was a careful biker. He'd done all the stupid things and survived unscathed. He'd walked away from one crash: Friday night foolishness among equally intoxicated friends. Bob still limped. But even in his foolhardy days Mike had held a respect for the moorland roads, a legacy, perhaps, of growing up in the country. Foggy December after dark was not the best time to negotiate the cattle grids and curves of the Bowland fell roads, especially when a strange woman clutched at his jacket and his concentration.

On a safe straight stretch leading to a junction he throttled back, slowed down, and lifted his visor.

"Where do you want?" he shouted.

No reply.

"Where are you going?"

She adjusted her grip on his jacket. Mike shrugged his shoulders and began the descent. If she wasn't going his way, hard luck.

Far ahead another rider betrayed his position

by the hazy starburst of his headlight. The silver-white beam burned for a moment before the fog snuffed it out. Mike waited for the machine to pass him, but it never did.

He knew the road well, but such was the severity of the fog that he could only recognise familiar humps and bends as they came within thirty yards of his front wheel. As they descended, however, the moisture became more patchy and in places cleared his view for half a mile or so. When he could see well, he accelerated and the girl behind him squeezed tighter, a gesture that Mike interpreted as a signal that she enjoyed the thrill of speed. She was tempting him to take risks. She was too late. Five, or even three, years earlier he would have responded, but not now. If anything, he drove even slower than he felt was necessary. If she was a siren, he intended her to be the only one that he'd encounter that night.

He realised that he was living out a tale that would stand many re-tellings over Yuletide bars, and while savouring that realisation he dropped into a hollow, hit a dense bank of fog and braked a touch too sharply. The rear of the machine slipped to one side and the engine started a scream, but the tyre gripped again and Mike regained control. His pillion passenger had failed to flinch, a fact that Mike found more unnerving than the skid.

He realised that he was sweating as a gradient warning sign loomed up like a familiar friend. He changed down and leaned the machine gently through the curve that crested the hill. A sheep, devil-like in the Gothic gloom, jerked onto the embankment as if fearful that the headlight might restore it to dust. It was a useful reminder that the road was unfenced. Not all demons were on her side.

With the machine under control Mike realised that he was equally vulnerable to a racing mind. Something as simple as her silence made her mysterious and nudged his imagination towards a higher gear. The flying frozen fog had made short work of his leathers and performed its peculiar sanitising of his skin so that, despite the barriers between, her arm against his belly was mere bone.

He gear-changed down both bike and brain and cruised through the close farm buildings at Sykes. They were on the civilisation road. More junctions now, but he made no further attempts to consult her. His route was clear, she may have come to claim him, but with his destination nearing he held her as his prize. The river ran unseen beyond the stone wall that formed a clearer boundary to the road ahead. He opened the throttle wider. Suddenly the girl hammered on his arm and he slowed to a stop.

She got off and walked ahead on the right-hand side of the road without removing her helmet. He eased his machine forward and immediately the unsteady headlight beam flashed on a gatepost.

When alongside her he yelled, "This all right then?"

She ignored him and cut up the path, leaving the gate to jar itself shut. Beyond her, on the boundary of visibility, Mike could make out the farmhouse that he knew was there. He had the option of riding another ten yards and cutting up the farm drive to overtake her, but didn't.

He could detect no light from the building and it was impossible to tell when she reached it, her slender form already having blended with the fog. He waited for a long time hoping for a sign of life in the house or on the path. Cars passed. One driver saw him late and told him so with his horn. Even when she had gone, she held him in a position of danger. He kicked the bike into gear and accelerated away to slip over the bridge at Burholme and cut through the forest to the inn at Whitewell.

Parked cars cooled as their absent occupants warmed. Mike removed his glove and ran his palm over the saddle but the mile from the bridge had been more than far enough to chill the plastic of the pillion position. He heard the laughter of friends inside. They would be certain to notice his unusual mood and probe, but Mike had already decided that, like the girl, he would say nothing.

WAITING AT THE DRAY-HORSE INN

December 1982

It was the chink of the pewter tankard that caught her attention. She had thought that the bar was empty. Evidently not. The strange thing about it was that she was sure Walter, the landlord, regarded the pewter tankards as being strictly for decorative purposes. She had never seen him serve a customer with one in six years of working two nights a week at the Dray Horse Inn. She had grown accustomed to the various distinctive sounds of glass on timber, which was why she reacted immediately on hearing the unfamiliar noise of the pewter tankard.

She was re-stocking the shelves in the lounge

bar while business was quiet in the early evening after arriving fifteen minutes late as a result of driving carefully through the icy country lanes, and she presumed the man seated in the corner had been served by Walter.

He wasn't a regular, of that she was sure. His thick overcoat was buttoned up tightly and the collar was raised, although the central heating was on and he was barely six feet from the crackling log fire. She could not see his face clearly, and he, it seemed, was too preoccupied with his thoughts to glance at her. From time to time he would fix an anxious gaze on the door.

She finished stacking the shelves and spent a few minutes straightening the drip-mats and generally tidying the bar area. One of the pleasing things about working at the Dray-Horse, she reflected, was that Walter had not allowed the need to modernise to impair the old-world charm of the interior. She withdrew into the kitchen.

"I see we've got an early bird tonight," she remarked to Walter who was deep in his newspaper.

"Have we?" he asked absently.

"Special treatment as well."

"Special treatment?"

"A pewter tankard."

"What?" Walter frowned.

"I thought you kept them solely for decoration."

"I do." He shook his newspaper once as a sign of his agitation. "You shouldn't have done that. Now they'll all be wanting one."

"I didn't. I thought you had served him."

"If I had, he wouldn't have one of my pewter tankards."

Helen returned to the lounge bar. It was deserted. Over the bar, all of Walter's pewter tankards hung precisely where they always did.

It was a quiet night. This was usual for a Monday, but tonight it was especially so. Outside a fresh fall of snow danced in a flurry to settle as a clean dressing on the mud-stained roadside drifts. The few regulars who had braved the December cold as it came off the moors found Helen rather more pensive than usual. Some of them had known her for ten years when she stood on their side of the bar with the young bank clerk who eventually became her fiancée and tonight was at home with their young son and daughter. Some of them were concerned by her mood. She was not the sort of person to let her problems influence her cheerful disposition, so they quickly noticed the change in her.

Helen was indeed troubled. She was certain that she had not imagined the stranger in the corner. She felt too embarrassed to pursue the matter with Walter who seemed to have forgotten about it by eight o'clock when he came into the bar to help and to chat to the regulars.

She remained abstracted for several days. She tried to recall a clear picture of the man she had seen but had to give up when she realised her imagination was taking predominance over her memory. She never conceded that she had not seen him, but as each day passed and she became more and more preoccupied with Christmas preparations, the memory faded.

Thursday evening was a special occasion. As a

member of the parish choir, she was taking part in a concert to be given to the residents of Bromington Hall, a historic, though modest, rural abode, now a care home for the aged.

Someone had the bright idea that they should provide an overture to the evening by singing outside in the gardens while the residents looked on through the windows at a picturesque seasonal spectacle. It was less pleasant for the wind-lashed choristers and a young man standing close to Helen remarked that the combination of double-glazing and hard-of-hearing meant they were probably available in vision only. Helen giggled and she chuckled even more when they were welcomed into the lounge and were warmed by the thoughtful provision of hot punch.

The evening was a great success. The choir rounded off their concert with Good King Wenceslas and were offered more refreshments.

"Coffee or Punch?" asked a lady with a dried-flower brooch.

"Punch please," replied Helen cheerfully. She was chatting with the young man who had cracked the joke in the garden. He was a new member and hence didn't know him well, but he seemed fun.

"Sorry dear," said the flower-brooch lady, we seem to be low on glassware. Hope you don't mind it in this."

"Of course not," said Helen trying to listen to the lady and her new friend at the same time. Absently she accepted the pewter tankard. She tasted the cool metal on her lips.

Somewhere a string quartet was playing.

There was the pungent odour of perfume and alcohol. A log fire roared and elegant ladies in full evening gowns danced by with regimentally precise men in spruce, tailed suits and stiff collars. Through the doorway Helen could see spotless footmen relieving new-comers of frock coats and furs.

Close by her a young woman and a man were holding a conversation. By the tone of their voices and the way their expressions contradicted the content of what they were saying, Helen realised they were trying to create the impression that they were discussing something much less weighty. She recognised the man at once.

"You will come with me?" he asked.

"Yes," replied the woman.

"You are - decided?"

"Do not doubt me."

"I do not, but it's difficult to believe my good fortune."

"Believe it."

Someone they knew danced close by them and they smiled. Then he said: "Monday next. I will wait until seven in the evening. If you have not arrived by then I will ride for Liverpool and sail for Ireland. I'll not trouble you again".

She sipped her champagne. "Where?" she asked. "Where shall we meet?" At that moment the dance ended and the there was a good deal of applause. The man raised his voice over it.

"At the Dray-Horse Inn," he said.

Helen felt ridiculous for having fainted.

spilled her punch down the front of her dress. She fumbled for an explanation but found it difficult as she was still reeling from the vision of the Victorian ball. "It was just one of those things," was the best that she could manage.

Mark, the young chorister with whom she had been talking, had shown considerable concern and he was quick to seek her out when the vocalists next assembled a few days later.

"I'm fine," she assured him.

"No after effects?"

"Only a bruise," she said.

"Oh yes?" he said hopefully. "Where?" But she chose not to enlighten him.

They squashed into various choristers' cars and set off to tour local country pubs and sing to raise funds for a hospice. They started at the Dray-Horse, where after a brief recital, Helen was soon the bearer of the heaviest collecting tin. Then they were off to repeat the process in as many venues as they could before closing times.

Eventually, the later hours of the evening found their little convoy straining its way up moorland roads to the isolated inn that was to be their final call.

"I've never been here," remarked Helen as they drew into the car park.

"Great place," said Mark. "My local."

"Local?" said Helen as she emerged from the car and scanned the bleak panorama. "Where do you live? In a tent?"

At the end of the evening, she stood alone side the pub, waiting for her car-load of nions to appear. The sky was clear and as a hard frost. The rising moon, big behind stunted black trees, glinted off the smooth wind-carved sculptures of snow. Despite the warm glow of the public house and the laughter of the folk inside, she became aware of her solitude, and the silence of the night.

Footsteps crunched in the snow behind her. "Did you know that this pub is haunted?" said Mark.

"Haunted?" asked Helen.

"Mmm," confirmed Mark, putting his arm around her and guiding her towards the car park. "By a young woman. She paces up and down the hallway. Legend has it she is waiting for a lover she'd arranged to meet here. Evidently he never turned up."

"Just a minute," said Helen, and she broke from him and hurried back towards the pub.

"What's the matter?" called Mark.

She stopped and looked up at the moonlit sign and read the name of the pub written there: *The Grey Horse Inn*.

HOME FOR CHRISTMAS

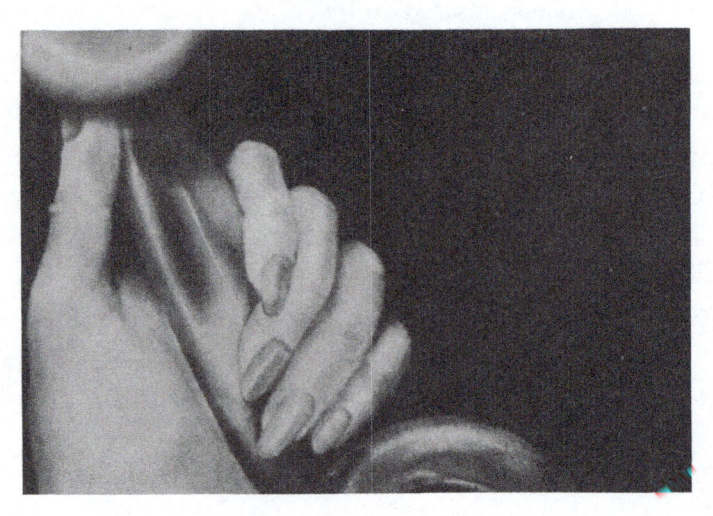

December 1983

The bed and breakfast project had turned out to be far more successful than she had expected. A surprising number of holidaymakers had chosen her home as a place to spend an overnight break en route to Scotland or the Lake District. Many, enchanted by the charm of Bowland, had decided to remain second and third nights, while others had pledged to return next year. Margaret was pleased. She enjoyed the catering and the company. As Dick had pointed out before they bought it, the house was large and remote.

Dick was often away, mostly abroad. Winning

orders for Britain as he put it. She had grown accustomed to it. Recently, however his periods of absence had become more prolonged, and with their grown-up family settled in other corners of the country, a flow of friendly visitors was welcome. But it was a flow that dried as the rivers filled with autumn rain.

It was December 1983 and they had had the house ten months; hence this was the first holly she had brought into it. She pinned some to the hallway beams, pricked by the angry leaves. She busied herself with the decorations. Busying herself was the key. That way her mind did not wander to small things . . . like the whispering she heard on the landing. The tunes the wind sang. It was the wind. She was sure of it.

She had adopted one of the rooms overlooking the rear garden for use as a studio. Here she plied her brushwork in the generous light of the French windows. She was an impulsive artist, never painting from sketches or from the landscape before her, but blending images in response to the urge of the moment. Many years of this creative pastime had sharpened her imagination and quickened its response to stimulus. Thus she reassured herself when lying awake at night listening to impatient fingers drumming on her dressing table.

So her days were filled with house-work, painting and the sanity of shopping. She made frequent trips to Lancaster and Preston, sometimes going on by train to Manchester and Liverpool. Anything for a day of bustle.

A week before Christmas she telephoned Brussels. It was an expensive call for it took them a while to find him.

"But you will?" she asked him.

"Of course. I told you I would." He sounded a long way off.

"You're sure?"

"Margaret, everyone goes home for Christmas."

"What about the Chinese?"

"They're very polite. They understand."

"I thought they were being stubborn."

"Yes, but politely."

"When then?" she asked.

"Not later than Christmas Eve."

"If it is there'll be little point."

"It's crucial, Margaret. Try and understand. Winning orders for Britain."

O come, O come Emanuel. It was the tune if not the words. And it wasn't the wind. She gripped the banister. Her knuckles matched the mistletoe berries. By the front door the telephone was still warm. Her husband's voice so far away and yet so familiar. A new voice now, strange, and so close. It hummed the tune softly, with a bright tone and a feminine quality. Evening settled upon her. She went to her bedroom and began to paint.

She put aside an unfinished abstract and stood a new board on the easel. She washed it completely in grey. She knew it must be grey. She had left the door ajar and through it came the rustling of skirts, ever nearer down the corridor until just beyond the door it ceased. A soft voice spoke plaintively.

"Make him come home."

"Splashed your car have I? Sorry." A warm smile split Mr Turner's ruddy face. It was the following morning.

"No. Well if you have, it doesn't matter. Needs a wash anyway."

"Messy job. Muck spreading."

"Yes." The tanker behind his tractor was liberally coated. "Mr Turner?"

"Aye?"

"Who used to live in this house?"

"Doctor whatshisname."

"Is his wife still alive?"

"Now you're asking," said the farmer pushing back his cap. "Now wait a bit, I'm thinking I saw her at Chipping show last."

"Who had this house before them?"

"Just previous you mean? Or what? How far before him?"

"That's the trouble. I don't know."

Not another coat of grey. Yes, it must be, but a ruddier grey, a dirty brown grey. She rippled it onto her picture, all the time looking for form, shape. She begged her subconscious to conspire with her brush, but they kept their secrets. It was evening again.

O come, O come Emanuel.

A distant solo. A carol singer. Carol singers. It had to be carol singers. She fled to the kitchen, grabbed her purse and raced joyfully for the hall. She flung the door open, but there was no one to pay. The song, as usual came from up the stairs, or on them. She closed the door, picked up the telephone and dialled Brussels.

"It's good, it's fine. I mean it's real progress." Dick's voice was faint. The line crackled like a winter fire. "I mean I could be home tomorrow, if it wasn't for the Germans."

"What about them?"

"Inflexible. C.J. is going to talk to them. C.J. will budge them. Bound to."

"I want you to come home Dick. I want you to come home for Christmas."

Dick paused before he replied. "Look love, why not cut our losses and slip down to Sara's? I could meet you there."

"I wouldn't impose."

"She is our daughter."

"Besides, "said Margaret, "haven't you heard?"

"What?"

"The snow. The M6 is a death trap."

Mr Turner stopped off a few days later. He left his snow-crusted gum boots on the kitchen mat and sat at the table while Margaret made him a mug of hot chocolate.

"Only ten minutes now," he said. "I want to have a look at my sheep. If it does any more, we'll be digging them out."

He had spoken with his grandfather-in-law whose testimony he now recounted, unfolding the history of the house's occupation. Before the doctor there had been the doctor's father, who had lived there since the nineteen thirties. Prior to that it had been someone to do with the cotton trade and before him – though here the old man had been uncertain – an army officer and his wife.

"So now you know," said Mr Turner.

"Yes," said Margaret. But what did she know? It was the women of the house that she was interested in, but she felt unable to press him on that matter. Instead she chatted about farming, keeping him talking as long as she could, savouring his company. The welfare of his sheep weighed heavily on his mind however, and he was soon slipping his boots on again. With a friendly wave and a cheery smile, he set off down the garden path, leaving her almost alone.

She went to her studio and viewed her muddy grey canvas. With a few quick strokes of black she laid in the position of some trees in the foreground, and one of two more in the distance. From this she established her perspective, then with various shades of grey she blocked in areas of light and dark and hence a shape emerged.

The snow fell outside the French windows, sealing her solitude. She felt a confrontation with whoever it was, was inevitable. She painted out her anxiety and begin to apply reason to what little she knew. Mr Turner's catalogue of characters was thin. Apart from that all she had to go on were sounds: the voice, the finger drumming and the rustle of skirts. The latter was an uncommon noise. That clue pushed the period towards the start of the century: someone in the cotton trader's family, or the army officer's wife?

By the time the light failed she knew she had before her a landscape. Broken trees, a trench and a battlefield.

It was the evening of the twenty-third of December; the day Dick should have flown out of Brussels. She knew he wouldn't even before he rang.

"It's this blasted freezing fog," he said. "Shut us right in. Nothing's taking off. Sorry love."

"All right."

"Fingers crossed. Perhaps it will lift."

"Perhaps it will."

He promised to ring the next morning or earlier if his flight was on. She put the telephone down and stood by it. It was a moment before she realised that the woman sitting on the stairs was staring not at her, but through her, at the front door.

She was a young woman, in her twenties. Her brown hair was gathered behind her head. A shawl was drawn about her shoulders, partially hiding a white blouse tucked into her long narrow skirt. She stared at the door as if she expected, or hoped, it would open and someone would come through, but at the same time she had an air of resignation that seemed to match that of Margaret.

Margaret was absorbed and suddenly unafraid. She sat next to the woman inspecting the detail of her clothing and watching her breathing, watching the life within her. It was only then that she noticed the small photograph in the woman's hand, the image of a smart soldier putting on a brave face. She knew that the soldier belonged not only in that picture but also in the one she had painted.

She touched the woman and was not surprised to find her feel warm and alive. The woman snapped her head around and stared wild-eyed at Margaret, seeing her for the first time. Margaret was startled but their gazes remained locked until both were calm again. Each understood there was no malicious haunting on either side. Something else had drawn them together.

Dick was profusely apologetic the next morning, Christmas Eve, but there was nothing he could do. The fog was still sealing Brussels. He was most disconcerted by Margaret's cheerful indifference and sounded slightly suspicious as he wished her Merry Christmas.

Margaret sprang about the kitchen all day preparing the most traditional of seasonal fayre. She cooked and ate it then – a day early. In the late evening she banked up the living room fire, poured herself a glass of sherry and drew two chairs close to the hearth.

As Christmas Eve became Christmas Day, Margaret and the woman shared the warmth of the fire. They talked. Mostly about timeless things.

THE COMPANION

December 1984

She smiled at the tricks trees play on the eyes, then the smile died. Her foot drew back off the accelerator and her grip tightened on the steering wheel. The engine protested and she changed down a gear. Her hair pulled at her forehead. The trees moved but the shape did not.

She passed close, cruising like a funeral, but edge-on the shape was lost among the charcoal lattice of the night trees. She pulled to the roadside and looked back at the place. Nothing but trees. It had only been a brief impression but it was sufficient to make her throat dry and her palms wet. She drove on.

She tried to obliterate the dark shape from her mind with thoughts of the town she had left behind. The bustle of solstice shoppers squeezed in lifts, and hurrying down the street trailing wisps of winter breath and hopeful children. Glowing window displays, carols courtesy of the Salvation Army, the Norway spruce in the square, the crib in the corner of the park, and swans on the lake like three ships sailing.

It was the only time of the year that she liked the town, when its grim impersonality was made jovial by a party hat of street decorations. She carried a little of its goodwill with her now, wrapped up and labelled and tucked in the boot.

Her parents and her brother lived on neighbouring farms which they ran as one. Her father was getting on now and while physically unable to do all the required work on his land, was mentally unable to stop. They kept some pigs and poultry but concentrated mainly on sheep.

Her father, she had no doubt, would be out on the fells even on Christmas morning. He would be there chiefly on principle but also because as much as he loved the company of his family, the fell was where he was happiest. He would look at his sheep and use the shepherd's minuscule vocabulary to send his dog sweeping through the bracken, sometimes to aid his observation, sometimes purely for the joy of seeing him run.

Kate hadn't visited her parents since September. She was looking forwards to seeing her old room again, doing the donkey work in her mother's spiced kitchen, donning sweaters and gum boots and walking the fields to help keep an eye on the pregnant ewes. Christmas on the farm was a time of celebrating one birth and praying for many more.

For a fortnight she would forget about books, the numbers on their spines and their positions on the shelves. The Borough Library was her choice, and in a sense, an ambition achieved, but somewhere in her soul, she knew she was enduring an exile. The flat and the flagstones would one day be no more than nostalgia. She belonged beneath the branches clustered for comfort in the folds on the Lancashire fells. She loved the country and was not usually disturbed by the shapes she saw in trees.

Kate was driving into a snow storm. Flakes, like ghostly moths, materialised in her headlight beams and hurried to collect on the windscreen. She switched on the wipers. Almost missing her turning, she recognised the junction just in time and swung northwards to wend her way into the loneliest parts of Lancashire.

The snow plough had preceded her, sculpting new verges and sowing salt to preserve its tracks. She hoped it had been all the way home for the isolation of her parents' farm meant they were often among the last to be relieved when the snow set its silent siege. The spirit moths swooping towards the glow of her headlights began a frenzied dance, tumbling hypnotic spirals that made her eyes ache. The road climbed and Kate felt the winter wind send rude draughts under the ill-fitting driver's door. She checked the heater controls. They were on maximum. Still she carried that dark image in her mind, in fact the more weary she grew the more it governed her thoughts. Tall, black and still. A man on a horse.

"Think of the town," she said aloud. So she thought of the town, but now all the shoppers had scarves pulled tight about their mouths; like highwaymen.

It became difficult to follow the road and Kate was forced to travel in third, and then second, gear. She knew which road she was on, but just where she was along it she could no longer be sure. She wasn't far from home, she couldn't possibly be, unless she had overshot the final turn off just where the road began its descent. Was she climbing or descending? She could no longer tell.

The snow whirled its enchantment. Her eyes burned. The dark shape rose up before her and she swerved to avoid it. There was a soft crunch and a brief mad screaming of the engine before it coughed and died. The moths' wicked dance had ceased. There was only darkness.

She stepped out into the blizzard. The car bonnet was lodged deep in the pile the snow plough had made. The wind scratched her face and she slipped back into the car where she found she was able to restart the engine, but try as she might, the car refused to reverse. The wheels span, scything out ever-smoother arcs in the snow. Fortunately, she recognised a roadside rowan and knew exactly where she was. Home was three miles by road or a little less than one if she crossed the field and took the path through the wood. She switched off, grabbed her woolly hat and scarf, locked the car and buttoned up her collar.

She scrambled over the wall and set off across the field. She was unable to exorcise that dark shape from her mind and she felt it was cutting a wide circle just outside the periphery of her vision. The blizzard renewed its malevolence by constantly shifting its frozen dancing veil and obscuring her view when she looked over her shoulder. The snow was deep and her ankles and feet were already icily wet. She grew to panting hard for with every step she sank to her shins and had to strain to free each foot.

The wood was unwelcoming. The trees whispered and nudged each other as she passed among them. Walking was a little easier for the snow was not quite so deep but she was already chilled to the bone and the cold in her feet was now pure pain. The blizzard blew fiercely at her back now making marble pillars of the trunks before her and piercing the knit of her hat to attack her ears. The trees ceased to be a wood and became a monochrome mesh printed on the atmosphere like a newspaper photograph. On she trudged for a long time, too long. She should surely have been through by now. Perhaps a little further . . .

She knew he was behind her and tried to run. Foolish. She should have realised by now that the snow was no friend.

She lay where she had fallen, face down. The highwayman walked his horse towards her. She heard the hooves through the snow, thudding in harmony with her heart. Pulling herself up, she staggered on, unable to recognise any part of the blurred landscape before her and not daring to look over her shoulder any more. Although saturated with cold, she was also sweating, and a solid wedge of pain was lodged in her forehead. The forces of winter were conspiring against her and she could not hope to win. The snow had made the familiar alien, had dressed every direction with the same disguise. Darkness hid all the distant landmarks she would have recognised and cloaked her from help. The wind cut into her, stole her breath, and left her numb. All the while she knew he was near.

She slumped against a tree trunk. Only a little strength remained and she would have to decide which way to spend it. She wondered how much of the night remained and longed for sleep almost as much as she feared it. Just beyond the corner of her eye the highwayman sat motionless on his steed.

A dog came bounding towards her through the trees and yelped with delight as he tumbled into her.

"Roy! Roy!" she screamed. "Oh Roy!"

Her father's border collie slapped his hot wet tongue about her face. She hugged him and he barked.

"Roy! Roy, how could you have known?"

He was an old dog and Kate and her father had long been aware that Roy knew far more than they ever would in certain respects. His arrival summoned a new strength within her and as she set off behind her new guide the ebony image of the highwayman seemed to withdraw. Whenever she stumbled, Roy sat by her while she regained her strength and struggled to her feet. Although impatient to get home he didn't press too far ahead, clearly understanding that it was important to Kate that he remained close. Soon he led her to a path that she knew well. She had to climb the kissing-gate for the snow had sealed it shut and as she tumbled off the other side Roy had vanished, but the warm lights of her father's farm were below . . .

Kate's mother treated her as if she were twelve, first giving her a sharp scolding and then almost weeping with relief as the full weight of her story sank home.

"I thought I wasn't going to make it Mum but..."

"That's enough," said her mother. "Half a tale will do for now. We'll have the rest when your father comes in." She made Kate dry herself off and sit before the kitchen range to await hot cocoa.

"Where is Dad?"

"Out on the fell. He'll not be long."

"In this weather?"

"He's been out for an hour every night, since..."

"Since what?"

"He's been feeling a bit – well, you know."

"What?"

"Well, he's bound to, isn't he? They'd been friends a long time, him and Roy."

THE HOUSE

December 1985

It was as if the house itself had shouted. He watched it hiding behind a veil of trees about a hundred yards away. He knew that in fact he had heard nothing and the shout had been inside his head but it was nevertheless something he had clearly sensed. It had caught him by surprise and made him swing around instinctively as if his name had been called: a grinding metallic chime, but heavily aspirated, like a voice. His binoculars were poised halfway to his head, stilled mid-movement as if by a photograph, and his eyes were locked on the house. He stared at it and the harder he stared, the more it seemed to be watching him.

He had been praying for moonlight. There was precious little nocturnal wildlife to be seen at this time of year and the absence of the moon made spotting it almost impossible. He had noted a few species of bird as dark had fallen and now, in the late evening he had been considering wandering home when a rustling in the undergrowth had caused him to freeze and peer and edge his binoculars eye-ward. Then came the shout.

The house stood alone, darkened and lifeless, and set back from the far side of the country lane. He raised his binoculars but they were useless, magnifying the darkness and blinding themselves. He began walking towards the road as if in response to a summons and it was only when he reached the field gate, that he questioned what he was doing. He paused with his hand on the powerful latch watching the house while it watched him and Pendle Hill over his shoulder watched them both.

Somewhere in the night a motorcycle roared briefly. He looked at his watch. It was time that he was returning to the village to put his feet up. There was another working day yet before Christmas. He wondered if he should mention the strange sensation to Emily, the younger of his daughters. She was just inside her teens and had often claimed to feel uncomfortable about that house. He'd always put it down to her imagination until now.

He opened the gate and stepped out onto the road, but as he set off homewards a shiver ran through him. Stupid, he thought, he'd walked past the house gates a hundred times before, mostly at night. He chastised himself again and again as subsequent shivers settled through him. He shifted his mind onto his hobby and the evening's disappointment. He thought he might have seen a fox tonight. Perhaps he almost did? The rustle in the bushes before . . .

The gateway to the house edged closer and he fixed his eyes on the nearest post standing sentinel before the bushes that hid the house. He tried to think of the Lancashire wildlife that he loved to watch but his mind leaped to speculate that the most interesting beast of all was the night itself, and this one was a rare specimen, cloaked with heavy cloud, yet thickly frosted. It had been still and clear, but a front was moving in. The darkness seemed to lie in patches that moved over each other when he wasn't looking at them. One of the gateposts had lost its adornment but the other was complete. Its lion's head roared at him. The carving, so grotesquely out of place amid the frost-clamped English night, seemed all the more strange as he couldn't remember noticing it before. It was at once both familiar and alien and he crossed the road to examine it more closely. In fact, it was a stone sphere and he wondered how he could possibly have seen it as anything else. Laurel leaf shadows cast by the moon perhaps? But there was no moon.

The house called again. He felt the vulnerability of a tired sleeper just woken from a nightmare and the danger was compounded by the fact that he found himself already standing on the drive without any recollection of a conscious decision to enter the boundary of the property. Sight of the house was like sleep to the nightmare dreamer: something both craved for and feared in equal amounts. He would walk a few paces up the drive. The garden undergrowth that flanked the drive thickened almost as if it were crowding in order to frustrate him. He heard footsteps behind him and turned to find to his horror that he was already out of sight of the road. The curved drive had embraced him with the unknown and each direction seemed equally forbidding now and as he knew that the curve extended past the house to return to the road at a second set of gates. He decided to steel himself and succumb to his curiosity and press on.

Although his daughter had long had misgivings about the house it had been empty for less than a year. Old Molly had lived there prior to that, visited by an occasional gardener and a cleaner, and her solitary existence had made her a legend in children's eyes, especially as she lived in the shadow of Pendle Hill, a place long associated with witchcraft. Her son and daughter had finally conquered her stubborn but inadequate independence and persuaded her to enter a rest home.

Suddenly the shrubbery on one side ceased and revealed frozen waves of a knee-high lawn and flower beds where lanky skeletal rosebushes pointed sharpened fingers at the house. The building was not particularly large with just four bay windows presenting themselves to the drive, and in this over-dark night the upper pair gleamed a little more than those either side of the door and he could not help but see the house as a face. An eye moved. There was someone in one of the bedrooms. He stared hard but saw only stillness. His spine tingled, insisting that there was someone behind him, but he refused to look. If there was anyone there they would have to tap him on the shoulder. He edged nearer to the house, the gravel beneath his feet chanting a requiem rhythm. The mighty gusts that high above his head slid the slab clouds over each other, moved gently down at ground level as whispering draughts, and as they stroked his face it was as if the house breathed on him. For some inexplicable reason he felt that he wanted the building to call to him again as he stood before it, to speak once more the grating slam in his skull, but it remained silent.

He began to have doubts and reason returned like a sensible schoolmaster making him consider that it was his head, not the house, that was disturbed. Work had been piling up and he was under seemingly ever-increasing pressure. Perhaps this was a warning that it was time to make a change, to consider alternatives. Christmas would give him a chance to think. A horse whinnied somewhere beyond the house. He was wandering carelessly now and a finger hooked onto his coat and pulled him back. As he freed himself from the rosebush another hand poked its stiletto nail at his eye and scratched his forehead. He stepped back, cursing, as the building breeze moved among the sharpened shrubs. He smelled dampness in the air: rain was on the way. He hastened for the other arm of the drive that curved away from the house to return to the road just as there was a vigorous tapping at one of the windows. He swung round and saw a movement at one of the bedroom windows, an indistinct wave. Perhaps the rising wind was slipping through the rotten window frame and lifting the faded and long unwashed net curtains? A salvo of iced stones hit him full in the face and an instant later all about him was being hammered white by a bombardment of hail. Instinctively he ran to take shelter in the doorway.

He looked out across the lawn and saw the landscape etched white, and for a moment he was distracted by the curtains of pearl shot drifting like mystical forces towards Pendle Hill, then he realised that his shelter was the wishbone porch of the house.

She stared madly out at him from the bay window. He jolted as if from the punch of an electric shock and stared back at a drawn face with sunken eyes and moving mouth. Her voice, if she had one, was drowned by the rattle of the hail that hid her just enough to allow him to still see her vague grey form. His eyes lip-read but his mind was no longer listening.

He acted without thought and soon found himself stumbling between hail and gravel away from the house. The rosebushes reached for him but he sidestepped and veered off to cut the corner of the drive by dashing across the overgrown lawn. The frozen tufted folds grabbed at his feet and brought him almost to a halt. The house threw its voice into his head. He scrambled back onto the path by which he had approached, and pelted for the road. The hail was changing sides now, shielding him from the house's stare, but then it stopped. His breath clawed at his chest. The garden foliage between him and the gate formed a black tunnel harbouring all the horrors of his imagination, but he sprinted eagerly into its ebony mouth. Shortage of breath made him slow as finger-bone branches groped into view and arched over him in a mocking guard of honour. A smudge of grey showed where the road was and as he neared he wondered if the gatepost would have its lion mask. He never looked and never knew.

The road was a river of tarmac down which he could drift to safety. He passed the second entrance where newer concrete posts held the wrought iron gates ajar in invitation. He jogged past them towards the first of the village street lamps, lying low in the sky like a guiding star at rest. He slowed to a walk and his breathing became more regular and his pulse cautiously settled, and with the sense of calm swelling within him came a realisation that made him stop and consider going back.

He hadn't recognised her. She had aged beyond old age, but it was her, he was sure. The sight of her was jailed forever in the front of his memory, and he watched her speak again.

"It's my house," she said angrily. "My house." Or was it "home"?

Poor Molly. Was she there alone? Did anyone know she was there? He ought to go back and make sure she was all right.

"What's the matter?" Jean gently toyed with the

tinsel as if unravelling her confusion.

"What's up Dad?" Emily pressed the remote button and an old Victorian woman mouthed Dickensian dialogue from within the silenced television. The telephone receiver at his ear chirped.

"Are you sure this is her married name?" he asked.

"Yes," said Jean, "but she might not be that one."

"There's only two in the book."

There was a click. "Hello?"

"Ah I wonder if you can help me. I'm trying to get in touch with Mrs Millcrake's daughter."

"Speaking."

"That's Gillian, is it?"

"Yes. What is it?"

He cleared his throat. "Well, I hope I'm not interfering, but I wondered if you knew that your mother was back in her old house."

"What, the old house by Pendle?"

"Yes. Only she seems a bit upset, and there are no lights on or anything."

"Don't be silly. She's watching television. She's here. She's spending Christmas with us."

THE GRAMMAR SCHOOL

December 2011

"You are no longer alive, but you do exist."

You can imagine the impact of hearing that. I feel, perfectly alive. Perfectly. Evidently, I am not. But I do exist, I have that on good authority, the very best authority, of a guru, a teacher, the best teacher, my favourite teacher, the inimitable George Thomas Tusk. George Tusk, or G.T. as we called him was head of physics at High Heath Grammar School, until one day in 1984 when fiddling with the fuse box beneath the Great Stair at the east end of the school he electrocuted himself and went perpetually west. Most found it incredible that an expert on physics should make such a fatal error and a veritable grassy knoll of conspiracy theories rapidly grew, varying widely from assassination to perfectly planned suicide. Now at last, I was the one who could determine the empirical truth, for he sat before me in his characteristic manner, on the desk, sporting tweed jacket, mustard waistcoat, white speckled crimson bow tie and, on his right hand, a wedding glove of nicotine stains declaring his eternal affection for tobacco.

"Was it an accident?" I asked him.

His legs dangled, twitching as if they were barely out of short trousers. The graffiti-pocked desk moaned in pitch-perfect harmony with the gentle scuff of his pendulum feet. "Can you remember your death?" he asked me.

I thought for a moment. "No," I said.

"Neither can I," said he.

"I didn't know I was dead," I said.

"Me neither," he said, "until someone told me."

"Who told you?"

"Einstein," he said. And for a split second I believed him, but then almost instantly – perhaps at the speed of light – I recalled that this was the kind of remark he would often use to colour the classroom banter and generate not only knowledge, but the very desire to know. Einstein shared a theory, Hooke extended his thinking, Newton would converse forcefully, and chats with Franklin were frequently shocking.

"Who really?" I asked.

He dampened the pendulum sway of his feet and pulled his sparkling pupils into misty focus. "Charming young lady," he said almost softly.

"Never seen her before or since." He glanced towards the three great towering windows of the classroom each of which framed the trees of the park into eight perfect rectangles. "Though I've looked for her often."

"Do you believe her?"

"Oh yes. It may take you a little time to come round to the idea."

"I suppose I've got plenty of that?"

"Never can tell," he said and slipped off his perch to negotiate the geometric lattice of desks and arrive at the middle window. "Some are here for seconds, mere seconds, others . . ." He drew breath. "Never leave." He punctuated this remark with a smile that was too quick to hide its despair.

"You want to leave?"

"Where would I go?"

"You just stay here?"

"It's a service. Now there's an out-dated concept."

"What about me? Must I stay here?"

"Who knows?" He shrugged his shoulders and went to the board rooting in his jacket pocket for a pink piece of chalk. He found it at the fourth attempt, and wrote *life after death* on the board. He rooted again and found blue chalk. He slammed a large Saltire cross over his question. "Never believed it when I was alive and certainly don't now that I'm dead."

I returned to my old desk and sat at it. "Then what are we doing?"

"Existing."

"But – how?"

"Breaks every rule of physics, I know, but I

think therefore I am. What I am is something I need to think about. And I can't think of any former student I would rather share the debate with."

"I bet you say that to all your former students."

"You're not the first."

"Who else has been?"

He half-sat on the master's desk so that his legs described a three-four-five triangle when viewed together with the table leg. "One or two," he said. "From your year."

"Who?"

"She didn't stay."

"She?"

"Still alive as a matter of fact."

Far away the Hunter Legacy grandfather clock struck a chime. I fought hard so that this new nostalgia would not derail my train of thought. "She didn't die? But she was here? Like me?"

"She died, or she couldn't have come. They got her back."

"Who did?"

Another distant chime.

"Medical people. Who else?"

"How long was she here?"

"Hard to say. Time and Einstein wait for no man." A third strike resounded from the distant hall. "That damn clock strikes every hour, but only ever gives three bells, and the hands never move."

"Then how do you know it's every hour?"

"Excellent question. I tried the Conan Doyle method. My pulse. But I haven't got one."

I gripped my own wrist and took some reassurance in the familiar colour and elasticity of the veins, but as always G.T. was right, for try as I might I could feel no pulse.

"So that method was no use." He stood up from the desk, thrust his hands in his pockets and faced the windows again. "But the sun does rise and it does set. It sets as it always did at the winter solstice."

"Over the spired dome of the cricket pavilion."

He spilt his face with the wide rubbery smile of approval. "Correct. Which enables us to work out the compass bearing of the pavilion from this room. Did we ever do that experiment?"

"Three times."

"Anyway, it was a fine December day and a half and I was able to keep a tally of Hunter Clock chimes between successive sunsets." He indicated the top right-hand corner of the blackboard where four groups of five and one group of four chalk strikes were arrayed. "Twenty-four."

A thought struck me and I went back to the window and looked out properly at the winter park. Everything I saw was twenty-first century, but swinging back to the classroom I noted that all was at least thirty, if not fifty, years displaced.

"Well done, Mr Moore," my teacher said. "Soon you will hear the sound of one hand clapping." That remark was one of his standard repertoire of verbal rewards. It refers to an aspect of Eastern philosophy in which the master opens the palm of his hand and invites the pupil to lead the way. He joined me and we watched a handful of people briskly striding down the avenue of the park, wrapped against the bleak mid-winter chill and treading on long-spent leaves beneath an overcast sky. "We are here and we are there, but they are not here. Remarkable isn't it. Fits in with a lot of fiction but with no recognisable laws of physical fact. Yet we have the evidence of our eyes. Or at least what used to be our eyes."

"Well, I'm seeing with something."

"Mmm. Can't be the eyes though, can it? Can't be the brain. Certainly not in my case."

"What do you mean?"

"I've been here too long."

"What about me?"

"How long have you been here?"

That question stunned me. I had no idea how long I'd been there, it didn't seem long, but more worrying was the implication that in some way time might be precious to me. "I don't know – a few minutes? When did I arrive?"

"Sit down, Ian."

I didn't want to sit down. I didn't want to stay. But where would I go and how would I get there? I sat down. At Simon Crawshaw's desk.

"As I've already intimated, we appear to be outside of time. You'll appreciate that for a physicist, that's very disturbing."

"It's not that reassuring for a journalist."

For the first time disappointment clouded his countenance. "Is that what you became? Mr Moore, what happened to the sciences?"

"For a while I was a technical journalist."

"For a while?" His eyebrows rose but failed to arch as if he were a marionette villain.

"Let's talk about 'whiles'," I said. "How long

have I got?"

He shrugged his shoulders. "How should I know?" He went back to his desk and sat on the edge again. This time the triangle was equilateral. "For ever, I suppose."

Something strange happened at that point. I think I must have fainted, though it's hard to see how you can faint if you haven't got a pulse or a brain. Then again, how can you think you fainted if you haven't got a brain to think with? The questions were piling up fast. The talk about time had instigated what felt like a cold sweat, but could neither have been cold nor sweat, I would have been short of breath but according to all logic I was not breathing, the room started to spin and for all I know the room might actually have started to spin, for I was obviously inhabiting, or at least experiencing, a very different reality.

High Heath Grammar School is a quaint bastion of English education. It was anachronistic even from its foundation in 1934. Initially, it was ahead of its time with many post-war innovations in place long before the war actually broke out. To begin with it had been extraordinarily liberal in its approach to instilling the desire engraved in its motto to *aude sapere* (dare to know) but the liberal staff were young and in times of war expendable, and as war would have it, were duly expended. After the war it reverted to the classical norms beloved by the lovers of wistful ideals and hence marched forwards proudly out of step with the continuous reformation of educational practice. Similarly, its décor clung to dusty leather, polished brass and stained timber as tightly as the ivy that bedecked its exterior gripped the deep red-brown brickwork. Corridors creaked beneath inadequate illumination. Staircase treads strained. Bannisters were punctuated every twenty-four inches with proud brass nipples so to emasculate any naughty boy who slid down them. Naughty girls only did so in naughty boys' imaginations. The assembly hall doubled as a gymnasium and had fittings to rival any renaissance dungeon, while the laboratories would not have seemed unfamiliar to Darwin or Lister. Carpets were rare but could be spotted in the studies of significant masters and mistresses, and it was while staring at one such carpet that my consciousness, if that's what it was, returned a moment, a few minutes, an hour, or an eternity later.

The atmosphere was three parts nitrogen, one part oxygen and one part cremated tobacco. G.T. was extinguishing a Senior Service cigarette in a brass ashtray fashioned by Martin Kemble when he was in first year metalwork.

"How long was I out?" I asked.

"An hour or so," said George Tusk. "Just under I think."

The seam on the red leather armchair was parting close to my right hand. I ran my finger along it to check that I could still perceive touch. The leather was cold, the straw stuffing beneath the open weld was much warmer. I realised that I could choose to breathe and took a deep breath. The airborne nicotine was sweet. "How did I get here?"

"You died."

"No – here. We were in 4A."

"You have no mass and hence no weight," he said. "How about some coffee?"

"Yes, I would like some coffee, very much."

George Tusk made me a mug of coffee and I greatly enjoyed the flavour. "What brand is it?" I inquired.

"Ethereal," he replied.

"What?"

"Like you, it has no substance. But it will refresh and invigorate you. You can drink as much as you like, this tin never dries up, and no, you won't ever have to go to the toilet again. Oh, and the cigarettes can't kill you. Want one?"

"No thanks. Do I still have to call you 'sir'?"

"You don't have to do anything ever again. But the 'sir' makes me feel at home. Don't labour it though."

"Well, sir, I have to say I don't really get all this."

"Me neither. But I think that's why you're here. Back to school. Learn all over again. And I expect that's why I'm kept here. To teach you."

"Kept?"

"I mean you plural of course. As I said, you're not the first. And I hope not the last. The problem is, I don't for the life of me know what to teach you, because I can't grasp it any more than you. That's why I rather hope you'll hang around and help me work it all out a bit."

"I'll help if I can, of course, but where do we start?"

"Where science always starts: with

observation."

The Hunter Legacy grandfather clock struck a chime. It was more muted than before. We were roughly equidistant from it compared to when we had been in the classroom, but George's study door made a tighter seal and softened the sound.

"I'm happy to observe. But you must tell me all you know. What have you told those who came before?"

"All I knew, which is not very much, but it provides a structure. A grammar of being."

A second chime.

"Okay sir, give me the grammar."

He took a small square green cardboard box from his roll-top writing desk and lifted the lid to reveal a pile of pills. "Extra strong mint, Mr Moore?"

A third chime.

"Thank you."

I took the mint and over the subsequent hours took lessons in afterlife grammar from my long-deceased teacher. I quickly learned that I was able to travel in a stereotypical spirit style in that I really could walk through walls, on water, or even in the sky. However, G.T. assured me that the novelty of doing those things would quickly wear off. I would also learn that there were much swifter means of getting from A to beyond B by simply enforcing a kind of desire to be at my destination. I would learn, however, that not all places and not all routes would be open to me. George was not able to say which or why, as these restrictions seemed to vary from person to person. As he had already demonstrated, I would be able to enjoy eating, drinking, smoking and so on, but although the sensations would be complete, the commodities would have no substance and no physical consequences. I could not take food from what he described as the 'primary' world, as this simply would not work. I would find that I could see, hear and touch l but not grip or move objects from there. My body and mind would have no need of sleep, though he warned me that there might come a point when I would crave it. There would, however, be periods of 'absence' such as the one I had experienced before I became aware of his study and they were unpredictable and instant. Nothing physical in the 'primary' world could harm me, but I could, and almost certainly will, feel pain.

I was placed on observation duty, and so took a laboratory stool to the window of the physics lab, which was adjacent to the 4A classroom, and perched upon it to watch the comings and goings in the park. The effect was a blend of the banal and the bizarre. The world beyond the window continued just as I would have expected had I been alive and out there to witness and be part of it. But inside the Grammar school, it was as it had been three, four or even five decades previously. By turning my head through barely sixty degrees I could swing between centuries. The Legacy clock struck three time and time again as I watched the park cycle through a night and day. I did not grow tired, hungry or thirsty. G.T. did not come to see me. Before night came the laboratory lights were on, and shortly after dawn they were off, but I did not touch them and I saw no other person do so. No one saw me. None of the passers by outside gave more than a glance at the college, except for one. One very important one. Very important to me.

She stared up at the school for a long time. It was morning, perhaps mid-morning. The minimal car traffic permitted to traverse along the avenue to service residences and businesses had ceased and the flush of foot commuters had finished. A few older children played football, a few more very small children were pushed in buggies, and a greater number of dog walkers exercised their captives. She stood alone. No child. No dog. No bag. Her gloved hands were mostly thrust into the pockets of her winter coat, but when she removed one to nudge her nose, I saw that she still clutched her car keys and so guessed she was not parked far away. There was something very familiar about her and yet also something very disturbing and I sensed the disturbance immediately on a deep level, via a kind of knowing I had not known before. I seemed to recognise her unfamiliarity and see it as something very familiar. She was looking directly at 4A where I had been the previous day and where from autumn 1983 I had sat four desks from the front and three rows from the window for the majority of my lessons. I moved a little from side to side, hoping that my movement would attract her attention and hoping against hope that she would in some way react to me. She failed to notice. There was something more than curiosity driving my action. I wanted her to see me, but at that point I didn't know why. The urge to attract her attention was very strong and without making a conscious decision I found myself moving out of the physics laboratory and back into 4A next door. I discovered I could do this without the use of the corridor or of either door. There I was in 4A looking out of the window, but she had turned and was walking away along the avenue towards the main road, towards the football stadium with its mostly empty car park.

It was this receding view of her that brought the recognition, the memory, the knowledge and the reawakening of a deep need. Her hair was shorter now, but still long enough to cover her upturned collar. It was two shades of straw lighter than the mousey brown of her youth. Mid-forties now, she was probably colouring it. She wore black trousers and small, neat winter boots. My hand was on her desk in the window row, second from the front. I knew the back of her head very well for she was right-handed and diligent, which meant she spent a lot of time curled slightly forwards facing away from me as she wrote reams of correct schoolwork behind a sash of fine mousey hair rimmed on sunlit days with a filigree halo. She was the industrious, intelligent, benevolent and dazzling Vivien Clarke.

Instantly George Tusk was alongside me.

"She was here."

"In 1984," I said.

"More recently than that," said he.

"What? Vivien Clarke was here, recently, like me? Like I am now?"

"Stayed less than an hour."

"When?"

"Recently."

I grabbed my teacher by his tweed sleeve, and found to my surprise, that I could grip both tweed and arm beneath in what must have felt like a most disrespectful assault. "How recently?"

The schoolmaster smiled indulgently, shrugged apologetically and then averted his eyes from mine to the fabric of his sleeve where it creased beneath my grip.

I let him go. "Sorry sir."

"Do you know Ian, it's only since I died that I have realised just how much we physicists depend on time. I think it's more important than space. What use is space if you haven't got time?"

I looked back towards Vivien. By now she was unlocking her car, a Volkswagen Beetle parked too far away for me to see clearly, yet I could see it perfectly well for now I was with her, or at least in her world, not too close but on the pavement of the main road that bounds High Heath Park. She was in the football ground car park on the opposite side of the road, unlocking the car, getting in, driving away, but in order to do so she exited the car park by passing very close to me. For a brief moment I felt she might have seen me, for there was a tiny explosion of great intensity deep within me and at the same instant her car veered, swerved and then recovered as she blended uncertainly into the traffic flow.

Someone almost bumped into me and as he stepped aside he apologised.

"Sorry mate." It was a man in a hurry.

"It's all right."

He was on his way. There was no doubt that he had he seen me. I sought out the next pedestrian, a mature woman laden with supermarket bags for life. We made eye contact and I nodded at her, she smiled polite anxiety and veered slightly away as she passed. So I was visible and tangible, but had Vivien seen me?

I knew I had the choice to remain in what George called the primary world and walk back to the Grammar School, or to instantly be there. I walked. I made eye contact. I talked. I did not risk conversation but exchanged "good mornings" and trite, brief comments on the weather. Some were genuine and civil whilst others gave slightly dubious expressions as they spoke, which unsettled me until I hurried inside and was instantly face to face with George in his study.

"Well, how did you find that?" He poured me a mug of coffee. I had no need of it, but felt I should not decline it.

"Weird," I said. "I expect it takes some getting used to?"

"Wouldn't know," he said. "I haven't been out much."

"Why not?"

He shrugged his shoulders. "Where would I go?"

Even in 1984 George Tusk had been lodged in an earlier era, a time when the Grammar School took a handful of boarders, and when some of the staff lived on site. G.T. had had a study and also a private room in the north west tower, that was cleared when he died, and never re-let. He was the last of the staff to reside within the walls of High Heath.

"When was she here? Vivien Clarke. When was she here?"

He drank his coffee, pretending that it burned his lip. "You're going to have to get used to the absence of the calendar."

"But she was here?"

"Have I ever lied to you?"

"How can I find her now?"

"Why would you want to do that?"

"I was in love with her for two years."

"Three decades ago."

"You just told me there's no calendar."

"She's still got one."

"I need to see her."

"Did you have a relationship with her?"

"No."

"Then what ever makes you think she'd want to see you? Especially now."

"I want to see her because she's been here and she's gone back."

"And you want to go back?"

"Don't you?"

He took two sips and stared at the dado rail. "I didn't particularly enjoy being there the first time."

I sucked a cautious breath across the brim of my cup, tasting the coffee aroma. "Is that why you took your own life?"

"Is that what you're telling me I did?"

"I'm asking. Sir."

He put his coffee on his desk and toyed with a pencil, tipping it gently end over end, and then he looked at me and smiled without engaging his eyes in the process. "I believe we are spared the memory of our passing for a reason."

"Believe is a strong word, sir." Thus I quoted back to him one of his own favourite phrases, which he used mostly in a scientific sense but also frankly whenever religion crept into what he called his 'experiential domain'.

"Are you still an atheist, sir?"

"Was I ever?"

"That's what you told us."

He swapped the pencil for his cup, ran his finger round the rim, lifted it to his lips and spoke across the surface of the liquid within. "I still don't believe in life after death," he said, and took a long gulp of coffee.

"So what do you believe?"

"That there are more things in heaven and earth than are dreamed of in your, Horatio's, Shakespeare's or anyone's philosophy."

The mention of heaven put Vivien Clarke right back in the forefront of my mind.

"How can I find Vivien?"

"You can't. Your only hope is that she'll come here again."

"I'll keep watch day and night."

He stretched out with his foot and straightened a haphazardly arrayed pile of books stacked on the floor close to his desk. "I expect she sleeps most nights," he said.

I did watch day and night, keeping a tally with chalk under the lid of Vivien's desk. There were a couple of occasions when I fell victim to the 'absences' similar to the one that I had experience shortly after my arrival. I have no accurate notion of how long I was deprived of consciousness at each instance but my impression was that they were brief interludes of less than an hour, but they frustrated me terribly, because she might have returned whilst I was not watching. Periodically G.T. would join me and we would use our joint observations to fuel the debate about the nature of our new existence. We did not get very far and I gradually grew increasingly disappointed regarding the extent of G.T.'s knowledge. Because he rarely left the confines of the Grammar School, he knew very little of what the afterlife was like beyond its gates, in fact most of his understanding of it came from persons such as myself who shared his residence for a while and ventured out. My refusal to go on more expeditions irritated him, and I realised that his need to learn was far greater than his desire to teach, but I could not get to the root cause of his reluctance to go beyond the confines of High Heath Grammar. Something out there scared him, and not knowing what it was scared me.

He feigned interest in post-1980s technology. I explained the exponential expansion of mobile telephones and how it was allied to advances that even as late as 1984 had been pure science fiction. He was aware of the internet but remained reserved in his reaction to its scope and benefits. He had watched the changing fashion of vehicles, of clothes, of personal accessories with muted interest. In discussion he reached for the holistic. He had no time for the functional ephemera. In fact, he had no time.

On the day of the seventh chalk stroke, Vivien returned. There she was, looking up at the school again. She was dressed almost identically to when I first saw her, except for her gloves, which looked new. She saw me. I know this because our eyes met and she froze, then semi-stumbled backwards and broke into a run. I wasn't going to let this opportunity pass and immediately put myself at the gates to the avenue so that I was there, waiting when she arrived.

When she saw me she stopped, froze, and her newly gloved hand went to her mouth where it stifled an inward gasp and then muffled an outward grunt. Her eyes burned into my face, whilst her face drained to the colour of the cartridge paper we'd used in art class. For a moment I thought she was going to faint, but within that moment she had ducked to one side and was running across the park erratically and with an awkwardness inflicted by shoes not designed for moving over soft grass at speed. I was terrified that she would veer off directly into the traffic flow of the main road, and so I held back. Once alongside the road, she reverted to a more normal gait, though still clearly in distress. There were other people about, and whilst she did not approach any of them, she seemed to take some reassurance from their presence. She kept looking back at the gate but I had moved my position, and though she looked round frantically as an alarmed bird might, she did not see me. This was because I was directly above her.

I liked my moving vantage point at the base of the December clouds. I floated vertically but looked down as an entomologist might when walking on a badly cracked pavement. From two thousand feet or less I watched her hurry to her car, get in and drive off. I followed her journey all the way home. So then I knew where she lived, and I also knew that she knew that I was no longer alive.

G.T. was not pleased with me.

"I'm not sure our purpose is to intimidate those who are still in the primary world," he said.

We were in the old Assembly Hall, bedecked in more timber than a Victorian frigate, and sporting once again the dangerously combustible navy blue velvet proscenium curtains donated to the school in 1951 by Edith Nelson, an old girl in every sense, not related to any descendant of the one-eyed seafaring hero, but an avid collector of Captain Horatio memorabilia nevertheless.

"Are you sure of anything, sir?" I asked with sufficient insubordination in my voice to rattle my former form teacher.

He lashed me with his look, then folded his arms and leaned on the stage which was conveniently raked to meet him at chest height. "I'm sure that morality is transcendental," he said. His fingers drummed a phrase of a hornpipe on the floorboards of the stage apron. "It is not a physical commodity. In the primary life and in this existence, it is a virtue without dimension, and I suggest, Mr Moore, that you employ it generously and in a positive direction." He sneered through his nostrils disturbing dust last animated during act five of *The Tempest*. "She was clearly terrified. I could see that from the Tower."

"From the Tower? Do you still use your old dorm?"

"The Tomlinson Tower. I use, as you put it, the whole school."

The Tomlinson Tower was at the north east

corner of the school, not where G.T. had lived, but where a spiral staircase coiled beneath mock Gothic arches to a place where I once tried to kiss Vivien Clarke.

"I'm going to visit her," I said.

"I advocate that you do no such thing."

"Well, I'm going to. I need to find out if she remembers being here, and how she got back."

"You're in my head," she said.

"Figuratively, perhaps."

"Literally."

"No, really. They can see me."

I nodded towards the other shoppers in the store. I had chosen my moment to re-join Vivien carefully and with patience. I had waited for her to finish work at the Town Hall and then trailed her through the city-centre market and the shopping centre, before letting her catch a glimpse of me between the lingerie rails of Marks and Spencer. It freaked her of course but I presented the most reassuring countenance that I could muster, and spoke slowly and warmly.

"Viv, please, don't be scared."

"But you're . . ."

"I'm what?" I said. She shook her head in disbelief and distaste, but said nothing, so I said "Dead?"

"I don't know."

"What?"

"I read in the papers . . ."

"Read what?"

She changed the subject. "We haven't seen each other in thirty years."

"You recognised me."
"Your picture was all over Facebook."
"Why?"
She looked over the lingerie quizzically. "You can't have..?"
"I can't have what?"
"Recovered so completely. It was last night's paper."
"Recovered from what?"
A woman in a sharp skirt and with so much make-up she could only have been en route to the service side of the cosmetics counter, overheard and bumped shoulders with an array of naked hangers.
"This is not a good place, I said. Want a coffee?" I couldn't believe I'd actually got beyond the grave before I finally asked Vivien Clarke to go for a coffee. She couldn't believe it either, but for some reason she acquiesced. Just my luck, she said yes when it was terminally too late. With a shrewd look in her eye, she suggested the café on platform three. I was happy to agree. Bizarrely she didn't speak at all as we made our way to the railway station with Vivien walking slightly ahead of me. Once on the platform she slowed and watched me from just inwards of the corner of her eye. I reacted to her glance with a perplexed squint. She led the way into the café. I leaned close and told her I had no money and wouldn't be able to lift the cup. She shrugged and nodded to the table in the far corner. I went over and waited while she bought and brought the drinks. Only then could I sit down, because until that point I couldn't move the chair from beneath the table.

"I'm not in your head."

She sipped her drink. "Unless you are also in theirs," she said indicating the waitress and the other customers with her glance.

I refused to engage in metaphysical debate and tried to get to the pragmatic heart of things. "So why was I in the paper?"

"This conversation can't be happening."

"Well it is. Please just accept it." I could see that she was oscillating between fascination and fear. "I mean no harm. I want your help."

"I'm not an exorcist."

"Why would I want an exorcist?" I asked.

"Sorry."

"I have died haven't I?"

She was about to take another drink but took a breath instead. "Well, what do you want me to do?"

"First of all you can tell me how I died."

"I can't," she said.

"Why not?"

"Because I don't know that you have." She looked sternly into my eyes, so I switched tack.

"Tell me how you get back."

"Back to where?"

"From where I am to where you are."

"How the hell am I supposed to know?"

I told Vivien all that I had experienced at the Grammar School, including my conversations with G.T. and the fact that he told me she'd been there. She said had no memory of anything like that happening to her, but at the same time she seemed to readily accept my account, perhaps too readily, so I put some pressure on.

"You're my only hope," I said.

"I can't help you," she said, and she drank a bit too hurriedly and her eyes left mine to restrict their range to the table top.

"Please Viv."

"Listen," she said, "I'm sorry you're . . . where you are . . . really sorry, but I want to ask you not to bother me anymore." She took one more gulp and began to gather her bags together.

That pierced. I put my hand on hers and gripped hard. I couldn't feel her, nor she me, but she stared at the point of contact as if it were a fatal rash. She stiffened but didn't recoil. "Is there any way? Is there any way you could have . . . been to the Grammar School?"

She relaxed in a tense way, and paused in her leaving preparations. She looked at my hand cupping hers. "I've got a heart condition," she said. "I was ill. My heart stopped. But fortunately, I was in an ambulance . . . and they got it going again."

"When?"

She brushed my question away with her free hand, and then withdrew the apparently captured one.

"Months," she said, and her stare sloped up and to the left into mid-air half way between me and platform three, and there she caught what seemed to be a difficult memory. "I can see the ambulance, the A&E department and the ward, but High Heath . . ." She dismissed the rest of the sentence with a shake of her head then started to gather her bags again. "Ian, if you, if you . . . are and you . . . do . . . well, this kind of thing, it might stop my heart again."

I sank back in my chair. She looked me

straight in the eye the way she had done when we'd been teenagers, with an expression of being flattered, of pity and benevolent rejection. I said, "Just tell me how."

"Sorry Ian, I can't." She stood up and walked out of the café.

I followed her, fielding an assault from the eyes of the waitress. Outside the platform was illuminated, the tracks running off towards green, yellow and red signals amid the dark of the December evening. The platform was punctuated with pools of commuters clutching clusters of store bags. Close to the booking office I caught a glimpse of a man dressed in Victorian style, and accelerated past him to catch up with my quarry.

"Ian, I'm serious. I really can't handle this."

We were side by side on the pavement ramp that led from the railway station. The diesel engines of the distant trains were mimicked by the closer but much quieter rattle of expectant taxis.

"I just need you to tell me a bit more."

Her effort was already making her short of breath. "What I can't remember, I can't remember."

"And what you can remember, you can tell me."

She stopped suddenly and for a pathetic moment I carried on walking and had to quickly regain my position alongside her. This generated one of those doubly awkward scenarios whereby a deeply serious situation almost demands laughter and the realisation of the same duplicates the desire to laugh. Neither of us laughed. She stood with her back against a billboard advertising the romance-enhancing potential of perfume. "You really don't know, do you?"

I lost my temper and used a tone of voice best reserved for more than a month into a relationship. "No!"

She turned back towards the station. "Platform three." She said.

"What?"

My skull resonated with the taxi rattle. Then she was gone, or rather I was gone, or the station, the city and the deep damp diesel-perfumed night was gone.

I regained cognisance in George Tusk's study. He wasn't there. The scent of smoked Senior Service cigarettes snaked into my nasal canal and a distant chime occupied the aural equivalent. All else was still. I counted the visible threads spanning one of the scars in the carpet. Five. Four butts in the ash tray Martin Kemble made, amid a dune and a half of ash. There were three fountain pens on the pancake-patterned blotter plus a set square, a protractor and a pair of compasses. Two pairs. A brace of pairs of compasses. A reptilian tail of a single shoelace hung over the brass handle of the middle of three drawers in the study desk. No George. No G.T. No one else but me.

After a minute, or ten, or an hour, or more, I set off through the Grammar School. I went in all the rooms, even those that I knew were no longer there, I walked in all the corridors, I went inside the Headmaster's study and saw the letter on his desk from Lovate, King and Bateson, solicitors. I went to the chapel, to the gymnasium, to the refectory to the lavatories where Kit Aldridge had won the pissing up the wall to the greatest percentage of your height competition, with an amazing score of one hundred and seventy-three per cent. He put his success down to the effervescent boost of American cream soda. I went to the Geography room where Sidney Cartmel had defaced the display map of the United States: Ida-whore, Mary's hand and Mouth Carolina. I went to the boiler rooms, once the centre of the black market in cider and cigs. I went to 4A and sat at Vivien Clarke's desk. No G.T. Just me.

I had some difficult decisions to make. Had Vivien been telling the truth when she had spoken of her heart condition? If so should I leave her well alone? If I went to see her again she may have another heart failure and then she might be with me for ever. Did I want that to happen? Yes. Did I want it on my conscience? No. Did I still have a conscience? Yes. Why? I had no idea.

All through the worst three years of teenage life, when puberty was in harness with romantic ambition, I had been hopelessly in love with her, but she had spurned all my advances. I had remained nostalgically in love with her and often thought about trying my luck again, but I had not seen her again until I had left her world. I ached to be with her. But then my conscience kicked in. What right had I to ruin her primary life, her secondary life, or both simply in order to satisfy my thirst for personal gain? Would it be love, or was I now replaying adolescence and confusing love with desire? I decided that I would leave her alone. Suddenly my existence was enhanced. This was Gothic love.

I went instead, in search of George Tusk. This would be a much more difficult task. Finding Vivien Clarke and haunting her was a piece of cake, but finding another ghost in ghost land was a technique I had yet to learn, however I had graduated from the mortal coil and gone back to Grammar School and I was determined to learn my new lessons well. I embraced my new timetable with the naïve unrealistic optimism of the fresher boy but where was my teacher? He knew the correct syntax of this after-language of existence. Was he now exercising his knowledge of tenses? Was he avoiding me geographically, or temporally? For I felt sure he was avoiding me. Why I suspected him to be guilty of such deception I did not know, but my suspicion was so strong that I gave it the status of knowledge. I knew that he was avoiding me and that knowledge helped because it led me to question why he would want to do so. The only answer would be that he was in some way uncomfortable with what Vivien may have told me. For the first time in this episode of my being I had the merest hint of a structure that may ultimately offer me meaning.

I circumnavigated and cross-hatched the labyrinth of High Heath Grammar again, but I grew swiftly dissatisfied as my theory that he was outmanoeuvring me became more and more entrenched in my mind. The world through which I now moved had altered rules of presence and it could easily be the case that G.T. had the capacity to move in and out of my chapter at will. I began to think rather more laterally and to wonder if there was a way I could demand his company. Was there anything I could do to make him return? I thought deeply about the appearance of the College. It was as it had been when I was a pupil, and I knew full well that over in the primary world, while the school still existed it had been extensively modified and refurbished. Also, certain sections destroyed by fire had not been rebuilt, yet here they were in my perception, exactly as they had been in my time, or more precisely in G.T.'s time. Things that I had seen changed after his premature death were here unchanged. This was how George would remember the school, not exactly as I recalled it. The structure was his construct, not mine. If he was watching me now, there was one place I could go that might just spark his ire enough to provoke his reappearance: the fuse cupboard where he met his death.

One of the main fuses was missing from its ceramic cradle. It lay on the tall physics lab stool that lived in the cupboard. The stool was kept there because the fuse cupboard was tall and had shelves at a high level. The stool served as an impromptu step ladder but also as a place to sit while blown fuses where re-wired using the repair kit kept on the shelf. The kit was on the shelf and the fuse was on the chair. This arrangement was not as was recounted in the local rag following the inquest into G.T.'s death. It had reported that the stool lay on its side and the fuse was found in the bottom corner of the cupboard beneath the fuse racks. George had fallen against the stool. He lay with blackened first and ring fingers of his left hand. The report said the empty fuse cradle was also dusted with soot but as I stared at it now it shone brass bright and bone white. The fuse on the chair was not in need of repair. It contained a large gauge of wire fit for fifteen amps.

George did not join me. Someone else did. There was someone else in the deserted and darkened college with me, but like George they were not keen to show themselves. I heard movement. I heard floorboards creak. I heard doors shut. I heard breathing. It's difficult to describe the terror of being a haunted ghost. I was a novice in a new world. I did not know its normality let alone the abnormality it might offer, and there was no place of familiar safety to which I might return. So how did I know the disturbances I heard were not made by the quarry I sought? I just did. It was as simple as that. I knew immediately and comprehensively that the source of the sound was not my favourite teacher. I also knew that George, like me, did not breathe. The only time that George used his lungs was to draw in smoke from his cigarette or blow cooling air across his tea or coffee, or as I did, to enable speech. The presence that I detected was completely different to the sound and the spirit of George.

I emerged from the fuse cupboard, positioning the door as George had left it - open. I went to the Great Corridor that led to the Headmaster's study, where we all knew the creak of the boards for they presaged a pat on the back, a lash on the backside or a horsewhip on the hand. There was no sign of my new compatriot, but there was a new scent in the air, or more precisely an old one, the great smell of wintergreen. Wintergreen was the perfume of performance. One of the sporting set had returned.

I had not featured in any of the school teams. I was average to adequate at most games and competition was fierce because, as with many schools of that type, sporting colours could make academic underachievement excusable. Boots, bruises and the aroma of wintergreen were certificates not only of approval but of elitism. I was being troubled by an elite spirit and I had had such a successful indoctrination with the grammar of scholastic glory that I was instantly guilt-ridden and filled with a sense of shame that I had somehow instigated the displeasure of one of the hallowed couriers of collegiate pride. So who was this gladiator of games and what, not on earth, did he want with me?

I heard him again.

I began to formulate a theory about who this person might be. There was a certain tribe that bonded via wintergreen and sports kit bags. Some were good at games, others were good at being in with those who were good at games and hence became good at making up teams. My tormentor was most probably one of that tribe, but from which generation? Would I know him? He was the worst of spectres in that he chose not to appear but rather to let me hear his presence. He breathed close. He tested the floorboards one tread before or after me. He closed doors.

So I now traversed the Grammar School in search of one phantom and pursued by another and saw neither. Eventually my theory as to his identity became more refined and spurned a related notion of a connection between my two evasive companions.

Alex Armstrong was an Adonis. He was the only young man that made me wish I wasn't hetero. He could have modelled for Michelangelo. He could have been selected for the England cricket team purely on his potential to shift cigarette cards. He was so good at games that his name was pre-printed on team sheets with spaces beneath where the names of mortals could be honoured by association. He excelled at academia. He won prizes for Latin, for History, for English, and for athletics, football, hockey and tennis. He was in the top set for everything and hot favourite for being made Head Boy from the day he arrived to the day that he was made Head Boy. He went out with Angelica West. And with her brother. I found him in the upper common room.

He sat in the moth-eaten, dust magnet that was the Luke Dredger armchair, a gift of the Dredger family in memory of their son who had been Head Boy before the war but failed to return from the Battle of the Bulge. Before we left, the chair was unofficially renamed the Armstrong armchair and, as I understand, it continued in its role as the common room residence reserved for Head Boys' bums until the great invasion of Health and Safety storm troopers condemned it to a November the fifth incineration between the peak of a pile of planks and the rectum of a fabricated Guy Fawkes. The chair was back now, restored in all its dilapidated glory and supporting with pride the pinnacle of High Heath intelligent masculinity. He, however, looked crestfallen, distracted and in pain.

"My lungs, Roger. Can you believe it?"

Roger was my nickname, as a consequence of sharing a surname with a movie actor. I didn't need to breathe. Alex did. He was compelled to take a succession of deep rasping inhalations followed by shorter, throaty and sometimes staccato exhalations. He looked gaunt and presented as a poor rendering of the paragon of fitness and male beauty his primary-self had been.

"What's the matter with your lungs?"

"Too damn good. The rest of me has gone but they refuse to give up the ghost."

"Gone where?"

"What?"

"Where have you gone?"

"Gone here old boy. Gone here."

He laboured. His eyes never met mine but locked their focus on the distant Common Room door. I tried to estimate his apparent age. He should have been the same age as me but he looked much older and younger. I remember hearing that he had died but couldn't remember when it was.

"How long have you been here, Feeble?" His nickname had been a sarcastic play on his surname and his physique. Now it rang cruelly true. I hated myself because I relished using it.

"Only just arrived."

"Then where have you been since . . ?"
"Since what?"
"Since you gave up the ghost?"
"Waiting to be unearthed, dear Roger. Waiting to be unearthed."
"What?"

But he had collapsed. He sat slumped in the armchair, still breathing, though more slowly, but completely unresponsive. I shouted at him, shook him, felt the absence of his pulse, and listened again to his wheeze, but I could not rouse him.

I began to wonder if all that I was experiencing was a construct of my mind. I had adored and despised Alex in equal amounts and here he slouched, the epitome of my ambition for him. Surely this was classic suppressed wish fulfilment? Could that explain all that I thought I had seen and heard? They said that at death your life flashed before you like some superfast cramming exercise in advance of the ultimate matriculation, but perhaps the saying was incorrect? Perhaps the final moments were splayed out into a virtual holiday where a version of one's hopes and dreams came true in the form of a macabre hallucination?

From over my shoulder came George Tusk's voice. "Break's over," he said. "Back to class boys."

And back to class we went. Within the sweep of a blink we were in 4A, me at my desk, Alex at his, me alert, he unconscious and slumped forwards, snoring with his head on folded arms, and breathing badly. G.T. stood in with his academic gown dappled by chalk-dust dandruff at the board. His cheeks were faintly pink, and his eyes were shielded by the glaze of mild embarrassment.

"So, what have we learned?" he asked.

"Nothing, sir."

"Nothing?"

"I am more confused than I was before."

"Without confusion there can be no clarity. Celebrate your confusion. Make sense of it."

"Why is Armstrong breathing, sir?"

"Life support."

My memory focused. Of course.

Tusk toyed with a stick of white chalk.

"He just wants them to turn it off." He touched the chalk against his lips as if it were a Senior Service. "I'm working on them."

She found me. I held fast my fast. I abstained from haunting Vivien but she found me. But firstly I learned George's method of evasion. I found that if I left the college and stood outside I could see all the parts of the College rebuilt after he had died and re-enter via them. I deduced that he must have hidden from me in a part of the College demolished long before I enrolled, but well known to him. I could never reach him there and now I, by going into the new boiler room built in 1985, escaped him. He could not get at me there. He could leave the college and look back and see it but the grammar of our new life meant that even though he knew I was inside, he could not join me. I could stay there as long as I liked.

I had leaped free from the lesson with Alex

Armstrong, though G.T. had raced after me and on two occasions had overtaken me to block my path and fix me with his stare of guilt and determination, but I had evaded him by sidesteps, one horizontal, one vertical. When in the boiler room I could review my thinking and did so for a minute, hour, day or week until an insistent beep-beep startled and summoned me.

I sat beside Viv in her ghost-white VW Beetle and she drove me slowly down the avenue of High Heath Park.

Her sweet voice had none of the uncertainty of our previous meeting. "Of course, it's a myth that he never leaves the Grammar School. He does it all the time, but like you he is bound by the grammar of your existence. Present tense is a development of the past. He can only inhabit the places that he knew when he was alive."

"I'd worked that out. That's why I hid in the new boiler room. How did you know I was in there?

"I didn't. But I knew you would be inside somewhere and I reckoned you'd respond to Betty's beep."

"So you have been there."

"Yes."

I settled deeper into her passenger seat, pleased, relieved, annoyed by her initial deception, delighted by her decision to find me, and pointlessly nervous at not being able to fasten the seat belt.

"I'd vowed not to see you again," I told her.

"Very noble."

"Are you being sarcastic?"

"Yes." She paused at the end of the avenue to

wait for a gap in the traffic. "Are you offended?"

"You bet I am. I thought it was noble."

"It was selfish."

"What?"

"Well, you didn't ask me, did you?" She punctuated that remark with pupil-to-pupil eye contact and suddenly both worlds seemed very good. There was a gap in the traffic but she didn't pull out. I wanted more detail.

"How much can you remember about your visit?"

"Not very much. I often wonder who's in there now. That's why I sometimes come and stare up at it."

"Ever seen anyone?"

"Oh yes." Another car drew up behind us. It didn't wait, but slipped by into the clear road before us. Vivien said, "He's collecting."

"Collecting?"

"Collecting."

"People from our class?"

"Some of them. And others."

"Why?"

"I'm not sure."

There must have been another car behind us, because this one too, now drifted past and pulled out ahead of us. Betty's engine chattered contently at idle.

"When you say 'collecting' you mean . . ."

"Killing."

I let Betty chatter a little more, and then said, "So can ghosts kill?"

"They can cause you to die." Viv sucked her lips and breathed deeply. "This is where I saw him."

"Who?"
"George Tusk."
"When?"
"There was the tightest of gaps in the traffic and I was in a hurry. He waited, then when I pulled out, he appeared."
"Appeared where?"
"Exactly where you are now."
"In the car?"
"My foot came off the pedal, and a silver Vauxhall slammed into the side of me. My foot went back on the pedal and I redesigned that regimental gate over there." She nodded towards the Territorial Army barracks. "I think they thought I was Al-Qaeda."
"Shit."
"It wasn't that bad. No one was badly hurt. I felt fine until about fifteen minutes later when the shock set in and I had a heart attack. Fortunately, by then I was in the ambulance."
"You were lucky."
"There's no such thing as luck."
"George caused it."
"G.T. tried to collect me."
"Why?"
"You'll have to ask him."
"So you came to your senses back in 4A with him?"
"Oh yes."
"And then the paramedics brought you back?"
"I brought myself back."
"How?"
"I can't tell you that."
"Why not?"
"It's not allowed."

"By whom?"

A white van came indicating the driver's intention to turn into the narrow entrance to the avenue. The driver paid no attention to us and swung wildly towards us, narrowly missing Betty.

Viv said, "I can tell you how to move on."

"I don't want to move on. I want to come back."

"Do you?"

"Of course."

"Why?"

"Well you did."

She smiled briefly, almost indulgently.

"Could I come back? I mean is it still possible? How long have I been . . . gone?"

"Time is not something you need to worry about."

"Isn't it?"

"They switched off Alex Armstrong's life support fifteen years ago."

"Fifteen . . ."

"His wife went to see a medium. George got through to her."

"Fifteen years ago?"

"G.T. is physicist and, just as when he taught us, he often pretends to be more ignorant than he is. I think he's worked out a lot about his reality. He also knows how you can move on, but I'll bet he hasn't told you."

"No he hasn't. Did he tell you?"

"I worked it out. It's easy."

"How easy?"

"It's a school, Ian. How do you move on from a school?"

"You get older."

Vivien looked at me with the compassionate disdain I'd seen so many times before so long ago. Then she smiled, and then she said, "You sit the exam."

"The exam?"

"It's very easy."

"You found everything easy."

"No really, it is. There's one question. And it's multiple-choice."

"How do you know?"

"I saw the paper."

"Where?"

"I'm not allowed to tell you."

I got angry. "Not allowed by whom?"

"By the rules."

"Then break the rules. I'd break any rule for you."

She giggled. "You broke a few in 1984."

I stroked her hand on the steering wheel even though I knew she couldn't feel it. "Not enough though eh?"

She smiled, then sank deep into a dark thought. "Are you sure you want to come back?"

"More than anything. And if I did, would you see me?"

She turned towards me and smiled with her mouth, her eyes and her soul.

And so I went back into the Grammar School. As soon as I entered the neo-Gothic porch I knew I was late. I could have passed straight through the door to 4A but decided instead to open it. There was a pleasure-pain in the twist of that cold handle. The brass knob sent fear and anticipation directly to the bowel. George stood at the blackboard, with metre rule in hand. He wore his sinister face, the one he reserved to signal severe and sincere disapproval, but now thirty or more, or many more, years later there was sharpened venom in his demeanour.

"Where have you been?"

Before I could compile a reply my attention was taken by the class. There were five of us now. Alex Armstrong was there, looking much better, in bloom again and not breathing or smiling, but fully aware. Mrs Hunter was there, the late widow of the late Headmaster who had presided over High Heath during my tenure. She looked lovely for a lady in her fifties, as indeed she had when we fifth-formers had fantasised about her. She was an off-screen goddess with the kind of fuller figure that refused to be constrained by any amount of modestly-styled couture. She sat at Susan Sefton's desk, and two seats to her left was a man whose face I knew but whose name I had never known. He had been seen in the school frequently, always in the company of members of staff, usually G.T., but he had never been introduced to us. He looked to be a contemporary of George.

"Sorry, sir," I said.

"Where have you been, Moore?"

"Absent, sir."

"Have you seen Miss Clarke?"

"Not for a while, sir."

He indicated my desk with his rule, and signalled his suspicion with his scowl.

I sat down, raised my hand, and when he

acknowledged me with a half nod, I said, "I want to take the exam, sir."

His scowl sharpened.

"You're not eligible," he snarled.

"Why not sir?"

"You're not ready."

"I think I am, sir."

Suddenly his face softened. "I'm trying to build a team here," he said. Everyone in the room shuffled with slight unease.

"What kind of team, sir?"

"A team to help me crack the codes of this domain; as I explained to you when you first arrived." I looked at Mrs Hunter and wondered how much quantum physics she knew. What kind of calculus was her predilection? I might, of course, been doing her a gross disservice, but in all my years at High Heath I had not had the slightest suspicion that the Head's wife's interests lay in any aspect of academia. And Alex Armstrong, though good at everything, was not especially interested in anything, except at being good at everything. George Tusk's friend looked like he might be very clever at cracking codes natural or supernatural, or simply just codes, but we others seemed a motley crew for solving ciphers of a paranormal kind. I suspected G.T. had more tenacious reasons for gathering us together.

I paused a moment as if in profound academic contemplation, then raised my hand.

George looked pleased. "Yes, Mr Moore?"

"May I ask a question, sir?"

"Of course."

"Why did you substitute your fingers for the

fifteen-amp fuse?"

His face fell. The class shuffled again. George's friend cleared his throat.

George said, "Well what do each of you think?"

I shrugged my shoulders whilst trying my best to signal my earnest curiosity, meanwhile Alex found great interest in the grain of his desk, Mrs Hunter toyed with her eternity ring, and George's friend observed the tiny specs of dust that rode the indoor thermals. When it came to the matter of George Tusk's premature demise there were as many rumours as the rumour-mongers wished to spawn. They explained why both Alex and Mrs Hunter might be there, and I suppose why George's unnamed friend might be there, but not why I might be there. Unless of course there were some I had not heard. I feared terribly what they might be.

George waited for us not to answer. We didn't answer. "Well, you are all wrong," he said. "You are all wrong and you were all wrong, but that didn't stop you saying what you said."

I couldn't remember saying anything, at least not until after G.T. had put a full stop to his life sentence, and I was going to loudly object, but then I could not be fully sure. My memory was not that good. Had I spread malicious speculation? Don't all schoolboys and girls? Could it have contributed to the suicide of our beloved physics master? I kept my silence.

"You were all wrong," said George. "And I shall explain just how wrong you were. But there are still some absentees, and we must wait for them. Only then will I teach you all a lesson. For the time being you can get on with your work.

The question is on the board. Do it in your rough books and be sure to show all your working out."

The question on the board simply said: *Why are you here?*

We all raised our desk lids in the manner of well-disciplined scholars and took out blue-backed poor-quality notebooks. George came round with pencils scented with the aroma of recent sharpening, then went back to the master's desk where he sat down and did some marking. I put my name on the front of my book and Vivien Clarke's name inside it. Vivien had obviously begun to work out what George was up to for she had hinted at something like this. She had also told me what to do and say. I was anxious to do as she had suggested but somehow found the self-discipline to stay and sit in silence. Five minutes, or an hour or three hours later, I looked up from the nine-line poem I had written. There was a sixth person in the room. It was Hilary Godstone, who had been God's gift to Grammar School gossip and widely known as 'broadcasting arse'. Never silent in my memory, she was silent now and sat before George separated from him by three rows of desks and twelve layers of embarrassment. I had never seen such a beetroot blush. She seemed to grasp her predicament immediately.

"Am I dead?" she said.

George huffed his way to her and slapped a rough book on her desk. "The question's on the board," he said. "I'm sure you'll have plenty to say." He jettisoned a pencil in Hilary's direction and returned to his desk with all the smugness of a successful dam buster bomber pilot. Hilary had been a thorn in everyone's side. She could turn the most feeble chit-chat into fatal sound bites. I was convinced now that Vivien had been right. George was not trying to solve the theory of supernatural relativity but gathering a clan in his own treacherous Glen Coe. This was about revenge. But what would the endgame be? Could it be the worst endgame of all: a game without end? Was he, as Vivien had implied, gathering a form to detain in perpetual purgatory?

I returned my attention to my rough book and turned over a new rough leaf. On a clean page I wrote a farewell note to George Tusk. I told him that he had been my favourite teacher and that I had been truly sorry that he had felt the need to end his mortal career prematurely. I said I was sorry that he felt constrained to remain in suspended education, between worlds. I wished him well and hoped that soon he would see his way to everlasting promotion. Then, leaving my book open on my desk, I stood up, and without asking to be excused, I left 4A for the last time, and went to find the Examination Prefect. I knew where she would be. Vivien Clarke had told me.

She was on the second landing of the Great Staircase. She seemed slightly too tall, as if her torso was elongated beneath her academic gown. She had the posture of a ballerina and the countenance of a pre-Raphaelite muse. She stood by a cherry-wood lectern decorated with carved cherubs, vines and scarab beetles.

"Name?" she demanded.

"Moore, Ian."

She put a tick next to my name on her register. Her pen was silver, tasselled, and embossed with Arts and Crafts emblems. I wanted her to look at me but at the same time I feared her pupil power would probably reduce me to ecclesiastical dust. She didn't look at me and I loved and hated her for that.

She said, "Do you wish to remain, to move on, or to go back?"

"I wish to go back."

She took the single velum of my examination paper from her lectern, handed it to me, and indicated with sacristan choreography an alcove in the Great Staircase, which enclosed a single seat and desk. I sat at the desk and read my exam. Exactly as Vivien had foretold, I saw a single question with three alternative answers. I also saw the warning against cheating, and the consequences, and realised immediately what Vivien had done.

And so I have something in common with my favourite teacher. Everyone thought my death had been a suicide attempt. If only they had known that I had long decided that no matter how unbalanced I became I would not end my own life in a way that involved inconveniencing others. Jumping off motorway bridges ruined people's holiday journeys and throwing oneself in front of trains made innocent people late. I would not do it. How then had I ended up in front of a train? And having so perilously positioned myself how had I ended up alive? Well, to be fair, I was only just alive, and for three days it was touch and go. But I came through. On the third day I rose again, or at least my eyelids did. The train, as it turned out, was not travelling very fast, because my suspected suicide was off the edge of platform three, just as the ten twenty-four was gliding to a halt at ten twenty-one. Its speed was less than ten miles per hour, but its weight was more than two hundred tons. I should have died, and had I fallen upon, rather than between, the rails, I most certainly would have. Under those circumstances I could not have escaped the Grammar School by earning a return ticket courtesy of Vivien. Courtesy is a most inadequate word. Generosity is a far too mean a word. Self-sacrifice does not come near. She gave beyond life, beyond love.

She kept her promise to see me again. I don't know how she did it. She must have charmed, or pleaded, or cajoled or even, in some way I will never understand, purchased permission to return for just a few minutes and keep the date.

My recovery was slow. I was in hospital for three weeks. They had to keep a close eye on my lower spine. I'd also had some trauma to my skull. All that could have explained my visions of the Grammar School, were it not that Vivien came to see me, long after I had gone home. For ages I mused over what might or might not have occurred, but I was in no doubt as to why it had happened. The memory of the accident itself has remained mercifully absent, but from the day I came round I could fully recall what led up to it, though until now I have not told anyone. In the weeks prior to the incident, I'd started catching glimpses of people who I mistook for George

Tusk. To begin with it was no more than that. I'd pass someone in the street, think it was him, turn to check and find that he'd gone. Initially I thought it was just my memory playing tricks, or simply that I'd seen someone resembling the George I remembered, but then it happened with increasing frequency, and at that point it became frightening. Then one evening, I was on the way to meet with work colleagues in the city centre, when he stood before me with such suddenness and ferocity that I cracked into an instant sweat and called out. For the remainder of the evening, I wasn't myself as we sat talking and drinking. I didn't confess what I thought to be a delusion and consequently my odd demeanour later fuelled the speculation about a suicide attempt. I'd deliberately left my car at home with the intention of catching the last train, but my mood prompted me to cut the night short and aim for the ten twenty-four. As it pulled into the station, George Tusk whispered a long-forgotten phrase in my ear. I turned to see him, recoiled, and backed right off the edge of the platform.

As Christmas drew close, I drove past the skull-like houses edging metropolitan suburbia and up onto the moors. I went into the Dray-Horse, the place where I'd always dreamed of taking Vivien on a date. I ordered a non-alcoholic beer and tried to savour the grainy taste. It was early evening and the pub was quiet to begin with but the food on offer had a reputation as good as the smell that came from the kitchen and trade picked up. Periodically I slipped outside, shivering past the smokers to the car park and the garden used for summer weddings. A border collie came to see me, wagged a smile, accepted my affectionate ruffle behind its ears, then stiffened, heard something I could never hear, and went galloping away. After my fourth sojourn I was about to call it quits and head for home, but there she stood in the pergola. Had it been summer she would have been surrounded by the scent of climbing roses, but the only aroma was the faintest whiff of iced nicotine, brought on the breeze from the smokers by the door. Thank God their brand was not Senior Service.

"You gave the right answer then?"
"You should not have told me."
"It's what you wanted."
"I wanted to be with you."
"Well, some things are not meant to be."

I gripped her hand. She removed the glove and let me imagine the warmth of her palm.

"What happens to you now?"

She took a brief glance over her shoulder. There at the far end of the pergola stood a tall man, he looked slightly too tall as if his torso was elongated beneath his academic gown. He was very beautiful but evoked in me all the ugliest of reactions. "I don't know," she said.

"But you have to go."
"Those are the rules. If you are between worlds and you give the right answer you can come back. But if you reveal that answer to someone else you will move on immediately."
"This is not immediate."
"It is where I'm going to."

"Perhaps I'll see you there?"

"That's not allowed. So don't try anything stupid to make it happen."

"You don't know that."

"I do. That's why they allow this one encounter. To let you know. We'll be for ever in different places."

"It won't stop the way I feel."

"The way you've always felt."

"That's right. How about you?"

She smiled. "I wouldn't want to spoil the delusion of a lifetime."

I gave a slightly hurtful look. Her smile amplified and became a chuckle.

"I wish you'd asked me out in 1984."

"Seriously?"

"Seriously." She kissed me for all of seven seconds. I felt nothing and everything. Then she said, "But our romance has always been, and must always be, academic."

GOTHIC REVIVAL

December 2021

"He thinks he's got a broken wing."

There was a pause. She thought she could hear other urgent discussions in the background.

"It is an offence to make a false emergency call, you know?"

"I'm not making this up. He's lying on the ground. He's got two large wings. He said he thinks he's broken one of them. It does look, well, kinked."

"Can I speak to the casualty?"

"I think he's fainted."

"Fainted?"

"Or worse."

"Is the casualty breathing?"

"He was."

"But he isn't now?"

"Hang on, I'll check." She crouched and plucked a small downy feather from the inside of the crooked wing and held it to the man's mouth. It shuddered intermittently. "Yes, he's breathing."

"But he's not conscious?"

"No. Hang on – he's coming round." She gripped the man's white clerical cassock and shook him. "Hello," she said. "Can you hear me?"

"What's the casualty's name?" asked the operator.

"What's your name love?"

The man looked straight over her shoulder at the mist-shrouded Gothic revivalist spire receding skywards to parapets where falcons sometimes roosted. "Peregrine," he said.

She told the operator. "His name's Peregrine."

"Peregrine? Peregrine what?"

She leaned over the man again. "What's your second name?"

He looked at the spire once more. "Walburge," he said.

She told the operator who sighed audibly. "And you said you are outside St Walburge's church?"

"Right next to the spire. I think he's fallen from it. Onto the pavement, it's a miracle he missed the railing."

The operator said they would send an ambulance as soon as they could, but stressed that they were experiencing a high volume of requests.

Moira crouched close to the man. She told him help was on its way. He looked confused, closed his eyes, and lost consciousness. She was about to shake him again, then thought she'd better not in case he had a spinal injury. She hoped the pair of wings, which were longer than he was, might have cushioned the impact. There was no blood, but he seemed to have stopped breathing. She began to panic and looked about for help. The mist was deepening. It was now more like fog. There was no one else she could see. She could hear cars, but they were some distance away. A train trundled by beyond and below the wall on the other side of Pedder Street.

"Peregrine? Peregrine – can you hear me?"

She took off her glove and touched his face. It was cold as porcelain. She gently stroked his head, and lifted one eyelid with her thumb. The iris was aquamarine. She shouted his name whilst staring into his eye. He did not react. She let the eyelid fall.

She looked for the feather she had used but could not find it so she plucked another, held it to his lips and then to his nostril. There was no hint of a flutter. Peregrine was not breathing.

She looked around once more. Still no one. "Hello?" she called. "Can someone help? Help!"

No one replied.

She found his wrist and pressed, feeling for a pulse. She couldn't even feel a vein. She fussed to find the buttons on his cassock. There were none. It was fastened with a cord. She whipped the bow free and peeled the fabric from his chest. The coils of hair which were blond, or possibly gold, lay static on an unmoving breast.

Right, she decided, spine injury or not she was going to do heart compressions and mouth to mouth. She was going to give the kiss of life to a fallen angel.

She had been trained in first aid at work, but that was years ago. She couldn't recall exactly what to do, or whether or not she should do it, but there was no time to dwell on that. She knelt by his head, ignoring the hardness of the pavement pressing through her coat. She opened his mouth, raised his neck, and gripped his nose with her gloved hand. She suckered her lips over his, and blew. The hairs on his chest separated. After three inflations she switched to heart compression. She couldn't remember what song she was supposed to use to help her get the rhythm. She knew it was a Bee Gees tune and opted for *Night Fever*. That didn't feel right, but she didn't dare to stop. She sang out loud the only words she could remember: *night* and *fever*. The rest she filled with 'la – la - las', belting them out as loud as she could in the hope that someone would come to help. No one came, but Peregrine came round.

"What – are - you - doing?" he protested, shouting in time with her beat on his heart.

"Thank God," she said. "I thought you'd gone."

"I had," he said. "You brought me back."

"Oh good," she said.

"You might have asked," he said.

"You weren't listening. You weren't breathing."

"I generally don't," he said. "Unless I need to speak or sing."

She stared and thought. Another train went by, heading towards Blackpool and accelerating. "You don't breathe?"

He began to sit up. "Not unless I have to. Why would I?"

"To stay alive," she said, suddenly remembering the resuscitation song she should have used.

"Bit late for that," he said.

She stood up and stepped back. "What do you mean?"

He held out his hand. "Do you think you could help me to my feet?"

"Of course," she said, noticing for the first time that his feet were bare. She gripped his hand, which felt slightly waxy, and pulled. He was a little unsteady and his good wing flexed and spread and he found his balance. She got a whiff of incense. "Are you . . . ?" she asked.

"Am I what?"

"Are you alright?"

"Not really."

"Then perhaps you should sit down."

"Just give me a minim."

"A minim? Or a minute?"

He broke into plainchant. "A minim or two will do!" He had a resplendent voice. He reverted to speech. "That's better." He let go of her hand and gave a smooth full beat with his good wing and an irregular swipe with the other. A few loose feathers swirled free.

"Is it broken?" she asked.

"I thought it was, but I think it might just be sprained."

"I've called an ambulance," she said.

"From where?" he asked.

"From the Emergency Services."

"You shouldn't have," he said. "They're under a lot of pressure."

"I wanted to help," she said.

He looked conflicted. In fact she thought he looked annoyed. He saw her disappointment and forced a smile. "You did what you thought best," he said.

"Should I just have walked on by?"

"You weren't to know," he said.

"I couldn't just have done nothing."

He realised his cassock was unfastened, tugged on the drawstring and tied a bow. "It's not your fault. I shouldn't have been here."

She noticed her glove and her phone on the pavement and picked them up. "Why are you here?" she asked.

"Too much ambrosia," he said. "Things are a bit hellish. Haven't worked for ages."

"Why's that?"

"Gig philosophy," he said, nodding towards her phone. "Everyone's got one of those. They don't call me anymore."

"I did," she said. "I called you back."

"Yeah," he said sarcastically. "Thanks for that."

"If I hadn't," she said, "where would you be?"

He beat both his wings and the loose feathers flew again. The weak wing was looking stronger. He thought about his answer. "Probably in trouble," he said. "I usually am. Well, blessed thanks. I owe you one."

"Forget it," she said. "For now."

His head cocked to one side. He could hear

something. "Your ambulance is coming."

"My ambulance?"

"You're going to need an alibi."

"Am I?"

He turned his back on her and beat both wings. His feet lifted clear of the ground. He touched down again and called over his shoulder. "All the blessed," he said, and whacked her hard in the face with his strongest wing.

All went white.

Time might have elapsed. The fog was now inside her head. She heard voices. They echoed.

"Concussed," said one. "Looks like she's been struck by something."

"All these feathers," said another. "You know your birds don't you?"

"Looks like a biggish bird," said the first. "Maybe a bird of prey. Peregrine perhaps."

Notes on the content

To Whom It May Concern
This story was first published in the Lancashire Post on Saturday 17th December 2011.

The Keep
This story was written in 2011 in response to reading of Charles Dicken's visit to Hoghton Tower in 1867 and his short story *George Silverman's Explanation* published the following year.

Pillion
This story was written for radio. It was broadcast on BBC radio in North West England in the winter of 1988.

Waiting at the Dray Horse Inn
This story was first published in Lancashire Life magazine in December 1982.

Home for Christmas
This story was first published in Lancashire Life magazine in December 1983.

The Companion
This story was first published in Lancashire Life magazine in December 1984.

The House
This story was first published in Lancashire Life magazine in December 1985.

The Grammar School
This story, written in 2011, was inspired by a number of Preston grammar schools. The characters were drawn from memory, imagination and indoctrination.

Gothic Revival
This story was first published in the Lancashire Post on 27th November 2021.

By the same author

Ice & Lemon

A novel

Not being able to get his luggage from the plane is the least of Dan's troubles. Heathrow is in a state of chaos. There are lifeless people everywhere but not one bears any sign of trauma or injury. Global communication freezes. London is gridlocked and burning. Mains power fails. Phones fall permanently silent. Life has simply stopped. Only those who were airborne when it happened have survived.

Ice and Lemon chronicles Dan's fraught expedition into a Lancashire blighted by extreme climate and thinly populated by desperate survivors in a frantic attempt to locate his family. What he discovers there could have truly cosmic consequences.

"An excellent novel. Stunningly assured, gripping from the off."

"Brilliantly told and full of humour and pathos, dealing with grand themes on a localised level."

"The story moves at a tremendous pace with shocks and surprises around every corner and a truly mind-blowing conclusion."

Untitled

A novel

She presumed their first meeting had been coincidental, but then discovered that he had already painted her in intimate detail. They agreed not to reveal anything about their previous lives to each other, not even their names. They became lovers and planned to marry, but then he disappeared and she had no means of discovering what might have happened to him.

A decade later she received a postcard that enabled her to start the search but, in doing so, she discovered that she could be the most hunted target of the Cold War. She hoped she could survive long enough to find out why.

The unseen and unthinkable escalating nuclear arms threat is the dreadful umbrella overshadowing this story, but there are other tensions here too, just as dangerous to the individuals involved.

National security vies with personal fidelity, integrity with identity, and nature with legality in this psychological thriller; and for the protagonist at the heart of it all is the perennial quandary: who really is the person that she loves?

"An exceptional mystery."

"The more I read, the more intrigued I became."

"This is a book I truly recommend."

Will at the Tower

A novel

He was sixteen, travelling with the most wanted man in the country, and hiding in the houses of religious fundamentalists. The authorities were closing in. The year was 1580, the place, Hoghton Tower, Lancashire. His name was Will Shakespeare or Shakeshaft. It depended on who was asking. Will at the Tower unravels the pivotal year in Shakespeare's adolescence. His adventures, his mistakes, his narrow escapes, his first loves, and most of all, the decisions he made that shaped his infamous future. It is the story of how the Bard lost his boyhood.

The Atheist's Prayer Book

Short stories in search of the super in the natural.

These stories are a quest to reveal the spiritual in the secular, the exceptional in the ordinary and the eternal in the momentary. Its blend of orthodox narrative and magical realism cuts into the darkness of misfortune and misadventure to intrigue the thoughtful and enchant the curious.

Strictly Done Dancing

Eighteen former celebrities step out one more time

A glittering selection of historical personalities are given another chance to dance. They have one more opportunity to show the world what their lives meant, but first they must meet their allotted partners and work out their routines. What will Fred make of Marilyn? What will Eric's partner think of it so far? Will Stephen's routine be out of this world? Who will dance with Diana? Will there be a winner?

The nine dances build on the biographical and parade through the celebratory, the sensational, the spectacular and the surreal. Each rehearsal is a potent dialogue exposing the hidden hopes, highs, lows, expectations and consequences of lives lived under the magnifying glass of public adulation.

Each dancer has an individual accomplice, but they carry the scars inflicted by a common partner who is as radiant as an illuminated glitter ball, and as sharp as a shattered one.

Papercuts

Short, sharp fiction

Papercuts is a collection of short fiction with deceptively sharp edges.

Here is a splinter that takes root, a girl who can see through her skin, and the true tale of a boy found thriving alone in the wild. Here is a location where moving house means exactly that, and where a vintage dress knows how to throw a party. Here are small boats amid beneficial storms, and perpetual trains to unlimited destinations.

These slyly surreal stories slice under the skin to sting the imagination. The majority were initially published in *The Lancashire Post*.

Great Hedgepectations

Can a hog have high hopes?

People say that the old woman who lives in the house behind the high hedge always wears her wedding dress and lives in complete darkness. This does not bother the hedgehogs who sometimes stay there.

Rip, a young hedgehog who is close to death in a graveyard, has no expectations, but the two girls who find him hope to change that. What they don't realise is that he could change their expectations too.

Inspired by Charles Dickens' novel *Great Expectations*, this is the story of how two girls set about helping an old woman and the hedgehogs with whom she shares her perpetual night. Rip, the orphaned hog, while negotiating the trials of hog's life leads the girls into danger, but also into a greater understanding of what the future might contain.

This story is suitable for adults and for older children.

Proceeds from this book, including author royalties, will be donated to wildlife charities.

ABOUT THE AUTHOR

Pete Hartley is a former drama teacher, fringe theatre producer and director, and author of novels, plays, short stories and some non-fiction work.

He now hawks his output under the moniker of *uneasybooks* and blogs as *uneasywords*.

He doesn't believe in ghosts, but is often haunted.